CORRIE'S

CW01521994

TRAFALGAR!

Corrie Wins the War!

Victory in dry dock at Portsmouth: photograph by Lance Croutear

ANTHONY BARTON

TRAFALGAR! is a work of fiction. Names, characters, places
and incidents are the products of the author's imagination.
Any resemblance to actual persons alive or dead is coincidental.

BULMER PRESS + ST. JOHN'S

2020 Bulmer Press Edition
Cover design by NZ Graphics
On the cover: The Battle of Trafalgar
Interior design by F + P Graphics.
Copyright © Anthony Barton, 2020
ISBN: 978-1-927721-36-0

PRAISE FOR TRAFALGAR!

'I cannot, if I am in the field of glory, be kept out of sight.'

... VICE-ADMIRAL HORATIO NELSON

'Lord Nelson's victory at Trafalgar was seen, first and foremost, as the final defeat of Napoleon's hopes of invading the British Isles.'

...TOM POCOCK, AUTHOR OF 'TRAFALGAR'
PUBLISHED BY THE FOLIO SOCIETY IN 2005

'When I follow my own head, I am, in general, much more correct in my judgement than following the opinion of others.'

... VICE-ADMIRAL HORATIO NELSON

'The silence on board was almost awful, broken only by the firm voice of the captain. "Steady!" or "Starboard a little!" which was repeated by the master to the quartermaster at the helm.

... MARINE LIEUTENANT JOHN OWEN

'Time is everything. Five minutes make the difference between victory and defeat.'

... VICE-ADMIRAL HORATIO NELSON

'The Royal Sovereign fought alone against five enemies for a quarter of an hour before help could reach her.'

...MIDSHIPMAN GEORGE CASTLE

'Desperate affairs require desperate remedies.'

... VICE-ADMIRAL HORATIO NELSON

'The wife of a petty officer took the wounded sailors up in her arms and carried them as if they were children.'

...AN EYEWITNESS ON THE DECK OF THE TONNANT

A Few Words Before the Battle

 I am so glad you have bought this copy of TRAFALGAR! CORRIE WINS THE WAR! Thank you!

This book could not have been written without the generous help of Peter Sargison, Honorary Secretary of the Chatham Dockyard Historical Society, and of Tony England, Fellow of the Chatham Dockyard Historical Society, nor without the unremitting efforts of Tom Pocock whose volume Trafalgar, An Eyewitness History, published by the Folio Society, has provided us with valuable insights into the Battle of Trafalgar as it was witnessed by the people who were there on the day it happened.

Heartfelt thanks also to Julie Wheelwright, who, in her meticulously researched Amazons and Military Maids reminds us that 'women served with the 'first-rates' during the Napoleonic wars, and 'performed a variety of jobs during the large-scale operations.' She goes on to say that 'A dramatic re-writing of history subsequently took place. In addition to women's long and diverse performance as auxiliaries within the military, the female soldiers and sailors were erased from the record or reduced to an occasional footnote. Those who were hailed as heroines, albeit exceptions a century earlier, became portrayed as amusing freaks of nature and their stories examples of 'coarseness and triviality.'

Let us try to put the record straight:

It is the 21st day of October,1805. The British fleet is standing off Cape Trafalgar. The fate of the United Kingdom hangs in the balance. Captain Corrie Harriman has just been called to Nelson's cabin. Corrie is dressed for the part, with her hair tucked under her hat. She looks every inch a male naval officer, but Nelson knows perfectly well that she is a woman, and that is why he needs a private word with her. 'This old coat of mine embroidered with the stars of my four orders of knighthood. I am a clumsy dresser. Can you help me? Thank you.'

As Corrie helps the one-armed admiral on with his undress uniform coat, she wonders what Nelson wishes to say to her, here on the very cusp of battle. Surely she is not here to help him with his coat!

They are alone together in the Admiral's cabin.

Nelson confesses that 'The reception I met with caused the sweetest sensation in my life. The officers who came on board to welcome my return forgot my rank of commander-in-chief in the enthusiasm with which they greeted me…When I came to explain to them the 'Nelson touch,' it was like an electric shock. Some shed tears, all approved – 'It was new – it was singular – it was simple!' and, from admirals downwards, it was repeated – 'It must succeed, if ever they will allow us to get at them!' One officer even went so far as to say 'You are, my Lord, surrounded by friends whom you inspire with confidence.'

Corrie looks Nelson in the eye. He has indeed been warmly welcomed, and she was among those who welcomed him, having been recently ipso facto captain of the Victory in lieu of the ailing Captain Sutton. But why has Nelson sent for her? And why now?

1
CHAPTER

'YOU HAVE SOMETHING to tell me, my lord?'

'Yes, Harriman. You were useful to me in our Battle for Co-penhagen.'

'Thank you, sir.'

'What do *you* think of my plan to take on the French and Spanish fleets?'

'I think you will surprise Villeneuve. Your general strategy is sound. Break their line in two places, hit them hard and preclude any chance of an invasion.'

Nelson continued to stare at her.

Corrie persisted. 'Why *am* I here, my Lord?'

Nelson lowered his voice. 'I like to plan for all eventualities. If I am wounded, I fear my friend Captain Hardy will go to pieces. The man is a dear friend but a sentimental fool. Don't tell him I said so.'

She grinned. 'He is very fond of you, sir.'

Nelson shook his head. 'Listen to me. If the worst happens, I want you to take my place. I want you to give the orders I would give. I want you to *win* this battle for England. Do you grasp what I am asking of you, captain?'

'If you fall, and if for some reason Hardy feels he has to leave the deck, then I am to take charge and win the war.'

'Yes. Will you promise me to do this, Captain Harriman?'

'I promise, sir.'

'One other matter. I want to make sure Emma and my daughter are taken care of, so I have written a codicil to my will. I would value your opinion *as a woman*.'

He thrust a parchment at her.

Corrie read the carefully penned words:

I leave Emma Lady Hamilton a Legacy to my King and Country, that they will give her an ample provision to maintain her rank in life. I also leave to the beneficence of my Country my adopted daughter, Horatia Nelson Thompson; and I desire she will use in future the name Nelson only.

Corrie shook her head sorrowfully. 'My Lord, you must know that with the recent change of government, and now that St. Vincent is no longer our First Lord at the Admiralty, neither Emma nor Horatia will receive a penny from those in power should anything happen to you. Emma and Horatia are both *women*. The men in government will overlook Emma's diplomacy. They will choose to forget that it was she who talked the Queen of Naples into writing to the Governor of Syracuse to secure supplies for the fleet.' Corrie took a deep breath. 'I urge you to stay alive, admiral. Wearing this coat sewn with emblems of knighthood makes you a target for French marksmen. Let me lend you a plain coat to wear instead. You and I are about the same size.'

Nelson shook his head. 'You have your orders, Harriman. Dismissed.'

Corrie left the cabin, shaking her head. *The obstinate fool has no right to be so damned brave. But then that's why we all love him, and I bet that's part of the reason why Emma loves him, too.*

As she stepped out into the fresh air she saw the horizon crammed with enemy ships. It was a terrifying sight. Perhaps nothing quite like it had been seen before in the long history of the world's barbarities. The wind had moderated during the night. Glancing back over her shoulder she could just make out four frigates, a schooner and a cutter joining the English twenty-seven sail of the line.

So now we are all heading straight for the enemy. It looks to me as if we are about to be annihilated. I don't suppose I shall ever see my mother again.

Moments later Nelson himself appeared on deck, his many embroidered decorations catching the early morning light, a brazen invitation to assassination.

'He is not even wearing his sword,' whispered Corrie's lover Lieutenant Tom Potts in her ear. Tom was the father of their child Nathaniel. 'He has dressed in his admiral's frock coat with those stars of his orders on his breast. I fear for him. Today is the day they hold the annual fair in Burnham Thorpe, the village where he was born.'

Corrie had to laugh. Tom had a keen ear and an analytic mind. She enjoyed his company. She replied carefully 'We had better give Nelson's villagers something to celebrate.' She looked again at the enemy ships, and added 'If anything happens to me, do not let your father electrify Nathaniel.'

'I'll try to keep him out of the laboratorium, but he is three years old, and he has the makings of a natural philosopher...'

'I don't care if he is another Newton, you are *not* to make his hair stand on end,' said Corrie. 'That is an order. I hope we both survive to see the little lad grow up.'

The pair looked one another in the eye. On the brink of what was promising to be a major engagement, there was little time left to say all that needed to be said, and little inclination to try. They both knew that they might never, ever see each other again, let alone their saucy little boy. But they were both naval officers. They had to be here.

A long, heavy swell was running.

The wind had veered and now it was from the west north west.

Suddenly something caught Corrie's eye.

She swung herself around.

She adjusted her telescope to have a better look.

What was the enemy up to?

She gave an exclamation of surprise. 'Villeneuve has changed his mind about making a run for Gibraltar. Look! He's trying to double back. I believe he has ordered his entire fleet to wear all together and head back for Cadiz.'

Tom sheltered his eyes with his hand. He stiffened. 'Corrie, they'll never make it. Not with this wind. We shall be at them long before they reach the protection of their shore batteries. Nelson has signaled that he expects every man will do his duty. What will his next signal be, I wonder?'

They both turned to look at Nelson expectantly.

Nelson turned to the *Victory*'s captain, Thomas Hardy.

'All ships. Clear for action, Mr. Hardy.'

When this new signal was lowered, the Royal Marine drummers began their drumroll and the *Victory*'s crew set to work with a will, tearing down bulkheads, screens and furniture. The portrait of Lady Hamilton was taken down from the Great Cabin and rushed to safe-keeping in the orlop. The gun crews checked their flintlocks and match tubs. Cooking fires were put out. Chicken coops and livestock, including the ship's goat, were slid overboard.

Corrie tightened her jaw. She hated to see the creatures left to drown.

I dare say the animals shall meet quicker, less painful deaths than we shall.

She watched Nelson make a note in his log. Then she heard him invite Captain Hardy to his cabin to witness that codicil regarding Emma and Horatia that weighed so heavily on Nelson's mind.

Meanwhile the ship's doctors, parson, purser and the loblolly men busied themselves with their bibles, bandages and medicine chests.

Sailcloth stretchers were made ready to carry wounded.

Battle was imminent.

Corrie caught sight of that muscular young woman from Little Sark who was serving as a member of a gun crew on the Upper Gun Deck. What was her name? Jeanette, that was it. She wondered how Jeanette would fare in the hours to come. Jeanette was a brawny miner. She had been rescued from her pit by Anne Keeper's son Fraser. The scuttlebutt was that Jeanette and Fraser were spending time together.

2

CHAPTER

WITH THE PORT closed, Fraser and Jeanette could barely see the gun lock they were supposed to refurbishing.

Jeanette frowned. 'So a flintlock has a hammer, a mainspring, a frizzen and a pan? At least working down the mine I was my own boss. I had time to figure out who I might become one day. What was like for you? You grew up in the navy?'

Fraser considered the question as he removed the blunt flint from the lock and replaced it with a new, sharp one. 'I did. I could sense how dangerous the navy was by looking in my mother's eyes. I knew Mama wasn't keeping pigeons for fun. Then when my Dad died…Woops! The tumbler. You forgot the tumbler, Jeanette. The tumbler holds and releases the power of the mainspring.'

'Show me how to half-cock. If you don't know yourself very well yet, then how are you going to know who to partner with? Who can you trust? Who can I trust?'

Fraser swallowed. When he was this close to Jeanette he found it hard to think clearly. He continued his lecture: 'The sear and the sear spring engage the tumbler, and then let it fly when someone wants to fire the weapon.' In a whisper he added 'When

I'm this close to you I want to reach out and touch you. I just can't help it. Lieutenant Tom Potts says there is a chap called Erasmus Darwin who thinks we all started from a single living filament. Perhaps what we feel for each other is just a yearning to be back to being that one filament again. What do you think?'

'I think the shape of the tumbler locks the half-cock position,' Jeanette replied.

'Wait for the click, then!'

'I hear it,' said Jeanette, and leaned back and shook her head to make her hair catch a ray sunshine that was shining in through a knot hole in the port lid. She did this to drive Fraser out of his mind with lust. 'So when I want to fire this gun, the flint strikes the frizzen hard and knocks off a tiny piece of iron?' she asked, and she pressed her face into the back of his neck to render him utterly helpless.

Fraser gulped. 'Yes, that's what we call the spark. You place a pan beside the frizzen with a little gunpowder in the pan waiting to catch fire. The gunpowder explodes, firing the gun. Odd that the French don't use flintlocks at sea. Their rate of firing is slow compared with ours. Abandoning all pretence, he pressed himself up against her so she could feel how aroused he was.

'I wonder if we shall ever be together,' she said, her chest rising and falling. 'Maybe we shall die before we have a chance.'

'Best not to think about it. Stop doing that, Jeanette, or the powder in my pan will catch fire. After the battle, we may be... different.'

'I hadn't thought of that.'

'You might have only one leg, or something.'

'Or no eyebrows. Or no... you know what.'

'One day one of Mama's pigeons came back without a beak. She wrung its neck. I wouldn't speak to her for a week. I was so angry. Peleus was my favorite pigeon.'

'Don't worry. Women are not supposed to exist. Maybe I'm a ghost. Can you love a ghost?'

Fraser sighed. 'I don't know. Sometimes I think I'm just a copy of my father, or a copy of what I *think* my father was like when he was alive. It is hard to figure out parents. They are part of the landscape when you are growing up. Suddenly I'm grown up too, and so are you. It's not fair.'

'Nothing is fair,' said Jeanette. 'I should know. I worked in a mine.'

'Let's refurbish the next piece. This is going to be some fight.'

3

CHAPTER

CORRIE took her eyes off the young couple. Preparations for the fight had been going on since dawn. Everybody had known when they woke up that something huge was in the offing.

At first light the men had been piped to dinner.

Corrie had watched the hands eat their parboiled pork and wash it down with half a pint of wine while the ship's band played 'Britons Strike Home.' She had listened to Lieutenant Bainbridge render the stirring words in a faultless baritone:

Britons, strike home! Avenge your country's cause!
Protect your King, your Liberties, and Laws!

At dawn Admiral Nelson had visited the decks of the *Victory* one by one, making the sailors on each deck laugh and encouraging them. Corrie remembered how pleased he had been with the way the men had barricaded the hawse-holes to stop any enemy sailors worming their way aboard through the ports intended for mooring cables. She had heard him advise the gunners to maintain a steady firing rate. A little later, after the Nelson had left the deck amid cheers, Corrie had watched one of the gunners chalk the words 'Victory or Death' on his gun, while another had carved a victory notch in his wooden gun carriage, presumably for fear that he might not survive to carve it later!

Now here was her *Victory* sailing into battle with her sails set to make the best of these light airs. There was complete silence. You could have heard a belaying pin drop. All eyes were on the unfolding drama ahead.

'Mama!' said a familiar voice.

Corrie looked down and smiled. Her three-year-old son was tugging at her trouser leg. Her little boy had sensed that something important was going on. He wanted to be lifted up to see whatever it was with his own eyes.

'I'm sorry, Corrie. He ran away from me,' said Corrie's father Lieutenant Archibald Harriman. 'Come on, Nathaniel. I'll lift you up. There! Now you can see everything the grown-ups are seeing. Whatever happens, the safest place for a toddler like you in the next few hours will be down in the cable tier with the other toddlers. Shall I take the lad down there now, Corrie?'

'Yes, father. If you don't mind? That would be most helpful. This is certainly no place for Nathaniel up here on the Quarter Deck. See you later, Nathaniel.' She butted foreheads with the little boy. This made him laugh. Of course he wanted her to butt heads again but instead she gave her father a nod, and her father left the deck in a hurry, carrying little Nathaniel in his arms to a place of relative safety.

A short while later, as Corrie's dad was making his way past the housing of the capstan on the Lower Gun Deck, ducking low so as not to bang his head, he happened to into Ramón Martinez, that Spanish lad he had befriended on the prison island of Cabrera.

'You look upset, Ramón.'

'Si, señor. I am at war with my own people.'

'I'm afraid that's true, yes. Your Spanish navy has joined with the French navy to try to kill us. But don't forget that both navies were complicit in marooning of you and me on that island. So we had better fight them both. How about I give you the job of looking after my grandson Nathaniel? He has a little hammock that the captain's steward Harbottle has rigged for him down with the rest of the ship's youngsters in the Cable Tier. Can you take him there? You'll know which hammock is his by his stuffed monkey.'

'Si, señor,' said Ramón, who was now in his early teens. He held out his arms to take Nathaniel.

'Very well. Make sure Nathaniel is bedded down in the Cable Tier. Can I trust you to do that for me?'

'*Si, señor*. I look after *el pequeño*.'

'See you later then, Ramón! I'll be getting back to the Quarter Deck.'

As Archibald returned to his duty station, the first faraway rumble of gunfire set the air in the ship trembling.

He set his jaw. The contest of arms had begun.

Archibald had attended the pre-battle briefing, so he could guess what he was hearing. Far off to starboard, Collingwood's column of ships, led by his one-hundred gun flagship, the *Royal Sovereign*, must be beginning to take enemy fire. Collingwood's column consisted in the main of 74s, but included also the mighty *Dreadnought*, of 98 guns.

Two other 98s, the *Téméraire* and the *Neptune,* were following closely behind the *Victory.*

When Archibald rejoined his daughter on deck he saw that she had put away her telescope, for she no longer needed it. They could all see the faces of the French and Spanish sailors.

They could hear faraway shouted orders, and the muted rumble of trucks as the French and Spanish ran out their guns. These sounds were growing louder by the minute.

Everyone on deck heard Nelson as he turned to Hardy and said 'I shall not be satisfied with anything short of twenty ships. We shall now veer to starboard and head for the middle of the line. Villeneuve is hiding there. I mean to surprise him.'

Corrie grinned.

Nelson sounds confident and sure of himself. I am encouraged. Perhaps we shall win.

Suddenly Corrie's friend Anne Keeper, the *Victory*'s spymaster, ran out onto the deck, looking flustered.

'What's up, Anne?' asked Corrie.

'Looking for a pigeon,' Anne replied, short of breath, and then, having scanned the deck hurriedly, she vanished down a companionway.

Corrie frowned. That was very odd, she thought.

Anne employs dozens of pigeons to send messages. Why make such a fuss over one pigeon in particular?

And then a strange thought popped into Corrie's head.

Perhaps Anne is searching for an enemy *pigeon.*

4

CHAPTER

CORRIE HAD GUESSED CORRECTLY.

Anne was taking advantage of the intense silence on board the *Victory* as the great ship bore down on the French. The vessel had become as quiet as a tomb. The only voices to be heard were those of Nelson and Captain Hardy. At this very moment she could hear Hardy giving a helm order.

'A trifle to starboard. Steady! A little more...'

Anne descended the wooden stair in haste, her mind racing.

I have to find a pigeon that should not be here. A pigeon sent by our enemies.

Every pigeon had its own distinctive voice. Anne knew the voices of her own pigeons, the bearers of her most confidential messages. She had named her birds after Jason's Argonauts: Mopsus, Orpheus, and Erytus. Mopsus had a high voiced warble, Orpheus liked to scratch about and complain, while Erytus made a soft, mellow fussing sound. Right now Anne was listening for the voice of a *foreign pigeon*. During these valuable minutes of intense silence preceding the battle, she had a rare chance to track down the strange pigeon she had seen fly *into* the ship through a lower deck gun port a few minutes earlier. If it was an *enemy* pigeon, and she was pretty sure that it had to be, then there would be a message tied to that pigeon's leg. Anne needed to know what that message said and, if possible, she had to discover *to whom that message was addressed.*

It went without saying that every vessel in the Royal Navy had an enemy spy on board, and it was part of Anne's job to identify the particular spy hidden in the *Victory's* ship's company. Unluckily for her, there had been a great many changes in the *Victory's* crew of late when the captain had recruited new hands from the isle of Little Sark.

In the confusion of recruitment some enemy agent must have infiltrated the *Victory*, someone who would be working in secret for the French or for the Spanish, and *receiving his or her orders by pigeon.* Every pigeon that reached that spy would bear a message. Anne needed to know what the *Victory's* spy had been ordered to do this morning, and who the spy was.

She had to find out in a hurry.

She dashed through the Middle Gun Deck, her head bent low. As she passed by the jeer capstan, she heard a pigeon croodle.

Rook-a-too-cooo!

That was not one of her birds. That was an enemy bird.

The bird's cries became louder and more desperate. The creature was in trouble.

ROOK-A-TOO-COOO!

The bird was in pain. It appeared to be hidden inside the cuddy of a seaman whose family name was painted on the canvas of his ditty bag:

D U P O N T

Dupont was the French-speaking able-seaman who had been familiar with Claude Chappe's telegraph code on the day when the *Victory* had sought shelter from stormy weather off the Channel Islands. Anne had suspected Dupont of being a spy when the cheeky fellow had been so glib about reading the signals of the castaways. She beat her palm with her fist. This was all her fault. She should have *acted* on her suspicion long since. Her failure to arrest Dupont had put all of the ship's company in danger, and now battle was looming. What mischief was Dupont up to? She trembled to think.

Whatever it is, I hope I am not too late to put a stop to his devilry.

She opened the man's ditty bag, peered inside, and there was the strange bird!

She removed the creature gently, her hand closed over its wings.

Yes, there was a metal message ring fastened around the bird's leg. Her worst fear was realized. The bird had carried a secret message to Dupont. Her thoughts raced.

The message is missing. Dupont must have read the message and now he must be busy obeying orders to sabotage our ship. We are all in danger, and I am to blame.

I have to find Dupont.

Quickly.

As she was replacing the pigeon in the ditty bag, she felt giddy. Something was amiss. She did not feel well.

The pigeon cried out one last time and died in her hands.

Poison!

Hastily Anne wiped her hands on her dress. The perfidy of the French and Spanish!

She closed and fastened the ditty bag, breathing heavily.

If I were my French counterpart, and I sent a secret message to a spy in an enemy vessel, what would I tell that spy to do? That is easy. I would tell my spy to set fire to the ship's magazine!

She thought of the faithful Perowne, the *Victory*'s Yeoman of Powder, slaving away below decks in his slippers among more than seven hundred barrels of gunpowder in the ship's Grand Magazine. Right now that meticulous and reliable fellow would be making up dozens of gun charges for the coming battle.

She broke into a run.

'Out of my way!'

She swept past a couple of midshipmen in her voluminous white dress.

She slid down a ladder to the orlop deck, facing outward like a true seaman.

Dupont sprinkled poison on his own pigeon! He knew I'd find the bird. So now I am poisoned. I feel ill. But I must carry on. All our lives are in danger, and I blame myself.

Down in the ship's Hold, Anne pushed past the queue of boys and girls waiting to be handed their linen bags of powder from the Filling Room.

'Perowne!' she whispered urgently. 'Are you there? I need a word.'

The hard-working Perowne lifted the hanging felt curtain that prevented grains of powder escaping from the Grand Magazine. He stepped carefully into the outer handling chamber. 'Yes, ma'am?' he asked, looking up at her, puzzled.

'If you were an enemy spy, how would you set fire to this magazine?'

Perowne scratched the back of his head. 'I'd enter when nobody was about and lay a twenty-yard slow fuse to a keg of coarse black powder.'

'Has a man named Dupont visited you recently?'

Perowne's cheeks lost their colour. He ducked back under the curtain and examined the stacked barrels of powder in the palleting flat. He reemerged, looking relieved.

'No foot prints, and no sign of tampering, ma'am,' he said, wiping the sweat from his brow.

Anne put her hand to the bulkhead to steady herself.

'Begging your pardon ma'am…' the brave fellow continued.

'Yes, Perowne?'

The Yeoman of Powder sounded apologetic. 'This is the ship's main store of powder. But what about the two ready hanging magazines? A spy could as easily put a match to either of those.'

Anne was shocked. 'The hanging magazines! I forgot all about them. I am not myself. Lock up here, Perowne! Take me to the hanging magazines. Hurry!'

'The lads and lasses will be wanting more cartridges for their guns,' said Perowne, gesturing to the queue of waiting children. He did not want to abandon his post with his work half done.

'Later, Mr. Perowne. We have little time. Do you trust me?'

'I won't keep you waiting,' Perowne said, and turned to the youngsters. 'Stay here! I'll be back soon.'

'Faster!' whispered Anne.

Perowne knew Anne well. Anne Keeper was the ship's witch. She had always treated Perowne respectfully, despite his small stature. Time and again Anne Keeper had brought good luck to the *Swift*, and now she would bring good luck to the *Victory*, Perowne was sure. So he would do as she asked. He stepped outside the Grand Magazine, locked the door with the key he kept on a chain tied to his waist at all times, day and night.

'Lead the way, Perowne! Take me to the portside hanging magazine first.'

Anne followed Perowne past the mainmast and the cable tier in the Orlop Deck where dozens of the ship's babies had been bedded down in tiny swinging hammocks to ride out the action, and came to the portside ready hanging magazine. Here the spare charges for the great guns were stacked up handy to the gundecks.

'I smell a fuse burning!' whispered Perowne.

'Find it!'

Perowne went down on all fours, following his nose. 'I have it, ma'am.'

'Get rid of the damned thing! Throw it overboard!'

Perowne whipped out his belt knife, sliced through the fuse cord, grabbed the live end and then threw the burning fuse over the side into the sea, to the open-mouthed astonishment of the crew of women and men who were busy loading their 32-pounder in preparation for the coming action.

'Taken care of, ma'am,' sang out Perowne, brushing the powder grains from his hands. He looked at her with new respect. 'Shall I check the starboard hanging magazine?'

Anne gave him her witching look.

'Foolish question. Checking, m'am.'

Moments later, a second smoldering fuse was tossed over the side.

'How did you know?' he asked, staring at her wide-eyed. Perowne had no trouble imagining the terrible explosions that might have torn the *Victory* in two.

'Go back to your Grand Magazine, Mr. Perowne. On the double! Fill those charge bags for those youngsters. Hurry!'

Perowne touched his forelock and darted below to resume his work.

Anne's head was pulsing. She was beginning to see things. The sounds of gunfire was growing louder. The poison was affecting her breathing. She was battling for her life.

She raised her voice to bellow out loud one of Newton's most powerful spells. 'They will then become oyles shining in ye dark and fit for magical uses!'

The gun crews gave her a cheer. They were greatly encouraged! Their witch was in action!

Anne cursed herself for an idiot.

Your witch is a dim-wit. What will Dupont try next? Where the devil am I to find this wretched spy? There are more than eight hundred people on board. How am I to discover a traitor among all these patriotic members of the Victory's *crew?*

She needed help!

She needed Corrie!

Corrie knew *every* member of her crew. She had last seen Corrie up on the quarterdeck. The *Victory* was sailing closer and closer to the French flagship. Nelson and Hardy must not be distracted at a moment as important as this, but surely she and Corrie could work together to track down the wretched fellow Dupont and put an end to him. Yes, *Corrie* was Anne's best hope. And best friend.

Holding up her skirts, breathing fast, her face streaming with sweat, Anne made her way back up the companionway as fast as she could.

She stumbled out onto the quarterdeck.

The wind caught her dress.

Thank goodness! There was Corrie, standing by the binnacle, talking to her lover, Lieutenant Potts.

Anne crossed the deck in a flurry of muslin and whispered urgently in Corrie's ear. 'We have to find an Able-Seaman Dupont. He tried to start fires in the ready hanging magazines. He will be planning something worse.'

5

CHAPTER

CORRIE took a quick glance over Anne's shoulder at Nelson parading about on his quarterdeck flaunting those embroidered stars of his, and her heart sank. If Dupont found a musket, then Nelson would not stand a chance. There were muskets to had everywhere.

Corrie threw Anne a shrewd look. 'Dupont's duty station is abaft the Surgery. We'll start there and work forward. Are you up to this? You look… out of sorts.'

Anne grabbed at the binnacle for support. 'I'm fine,' she lied through her teeth.

'Come with me, then!' said Corrie, and both women left the deck in a hurry.

Minutes later, Anne put her head into the surgery, a vein pulsing in her forehead. 'I'm looking for Able-Seaman Dupont. Have you seen him?'

'Not today,' said the Surgeon, without looking up from her dropper bottles. She was busy preparing doses of laudanum.

Norah, the ship's Scottish cook and the mother of twins, was making ready hundreds of slings and bandages. 'I know Dupont,' she volunteered. 'He's a Tarry Breeks that one. Keeps to himself.'

Anne left in a hurry, slamming the door behind her in her haste.

The slam of the door woke Corrie's brother Jim, who was a patient in the infirmary.

Jim tried to sit up. He looked about him, bewildered. 'We are preparing for a *battle*? Is something going on that I don't know about?'

'Aye,' said Norah, breathing heavily. 'We have sighted the French *and* the Spanish fleets. Never in all my days have I clapped eyes on so many ships all crowded together in one place.'

Jim gasped.

A fight in the offing? And me in Sick Bay? My gun crews will be lost without me.

He swung his legs over the side of the cot and began fumbling at the stupid bandage wrapped around on his head. He had to be on deck with his sister Corrie, who was as reckless and foolhardy as her friend Admiral Nelson.

Right now Jim was absent from his battle station on the Upper Gun Deck. His gun crews would be wondering where he was. More important, he had to be as close to the Quarter Deck as possible. He had to be nearby to seize command and make his reputation by giving brilliant orders. He had to shine in the eyes of his superiors. It was his only hope of advancing in the navy. He deserved to have his own command. Here was an opportunity not to be missed.

Why is my head so sore? Did I come a cropper?

'The French *and* the Spanish, you say? The French *and* the Spanish fleets have left the port of Cadiz? Doctor, is this true?'

'Yes,' replied Dr. Barry shortly, and the added in a more kindly voice 'You are in no condition to fight either of them at the moment, Captain Harriman. You have yet to regain your sense of balance. Far better that you remain here in sick bay where I may observe you.'

Jim's eyes narrowed. It was all a scheme to prevent him from showing his brilliance as an officer. He shook is sore head. 'If what you say about the French and the Spanish is true, then this sickbay will soon become crowded, doctor. Better get rid me of me now while you can. Look! I can stand. Nothing wrong with my sense of balance.' He staggered with the roll of the vessel and bumped into Norah. 'Sorry, Norah! Help me take this damned thing off my head?'

Norah was not about to do any such thing without the express permission of the ship's Sickbay Surgeon. She looked at Dr. Barry questioningly.

Dr. Barry racked her dropper carefully, climbed to her feet and stared at Corrie's brother Jim long and hard. 'How many fingers am I holding up?' she asked.

'Three. May I go now?'

He had to ask her permission. Here in the surgery, the Surgeon's word was law. Jim was duty bound to obey. It was a good thing that they were friends. By which he meant that he was privy to the fact that Dr. Barry's real name was Margaret Ann Bulkley.

'You may go,' said the Surgeon.

'Thank you, Dr. Barry,' said Jim, grinning, and left in a hurry, grabbing at a stanchion to avoid tripping over the coaming.

Trying to compensate for the motion of the ship, he hit his head on a hanging knee, and swore an oath under his breath.

Even the damned ship was trying to stop him from winning the war single-handed.

But he was an officer. This would not do. He had to behave himself. He had to show himself cool under fire, and clear-headed. He had to dream up some remarkable order that would turn the tide of the war and earn him a medal. Just like that! Then there would be an end to kow-towing to his sister, Sir Whatever-She-Called-Herself.

He staggered out of the After Cockpit, made his way to the Wardroom and flung open the door to the small cabin he shared with Dutty Boukman, the towering revolutionary leader of rebellious slaves who had been tricked by Corrie into joining the ship's company off the island of Sark. He found the cabin empty. Good! The *Victory* was eerily silent. What the devil was going on? He grabbed his sword, tried the blade, buckled the belt round his waist, and then dashed up on deck to see to those gun crews of his.

Breaking out into the open air, he was dumb-founded by the astonishing sight of three great fleets of ships making ready to do battle.

Merciful heavens!

He could hardly believe his eyes. He had never before seen so many ships on one place!

He made a quick tally.

By his count, twenty-seven British sail-of-the-line were closing in on thirty-three French and Spanish first rates, and all were accompanied by dozens of smaller vessels!

There was only one conclusion he could reach.

She did it! My damnably clever sister's ruse to bring Villeneuve out of Cadiz worked!

*He remembered how Corrie had contrived to send a false signal
to Villeneuve using the French system of semaphore stations.*

My sister has precipitated this naval battle to end all naval battles.

These twelve-pounders on the upper gun deck are my duty station.

'Gun crews! Lie flat on the deck!'

He prostrated himself, and called out to his sister's lover
Lieutenant Potts.

'Where have you stowed your little fellow, Lieutenant?' he
demanded loudly.

'Cable tier,' Tom Potts answered.

Jim nodded. It was important to show all present how wise
he was to be concerned about someone else's baby. His sister's
child would be safe enough in the cable tier. The young boy was
growing by the day. Corrie's steward Harbottle doted on tyke, and
Jim suspected that Harbottle was feeding Nathaniel a daily dose
of goat's milk from Captain Hardy's prize animal, but recently
consigned to the deep. His sister's child was a subject of much
sentimental conversation among the women and men of the
Victory's crew, many of whom had already stowed their own
toddlers among the coils of the seven great anchor cables where
they might be protected from flying splinters during the coming
action. It was by far the safest place Jim could think of to stow
away the young. Why Harbottle had even painted silver stars on
the deckhead so that the ship's little ones could lie on their backs
and look up at a 'night sky' in peace!

The gunfire sounds louder and closer.

A whiff of gun smoke tickled his nose.

Thus far all seemed to be going according to Nelson's plan. If
only Jim could seize some chance to make it *his* plan, to show how

brilliant *he* was, and give the Lords of the Admiralty an excuse to make *him* a Rear-Admiral of the Blue.

In the meantime, Vice Admiral Sir Cuthbert Collingwood, who was in truth a Rear-Admiral of the Blue, was at that very moment approaching the rear of the French line in his flagship *Royal Sovereign*. Jim sucked in his breath. Collingwood and his crew would have to suffer at least two broadsides from the French before being in a position to reply with their own guns.

Jim wriggled to the nearest gun port to have a look and try to confirm his suspicions.

Then he heard the whine of incoming shot.

'Everybody stay flat on the deck!' he reminded his people.

His gun crews had dropped the boards. That was navy discipline for you. No questions asked.

Most splinter wounds involve the upper torso. I don't want my people hurt before the action even begins. That wouldn't look good on my record as a gunnery officer.

A shot flew whining overhead without harming anyone.

Then there came the ominous rolling crash of an enemy broadside.

Jim frowned, trying to figure out what was happening. He focused his telescope on the other British column.

The Algésiras *is firing at Collingwood. She is commanded by de Magon, a truly scary French Rear-Admiral. I met de Magon once during the Peace. Perhaps the gunners in the Royal Sovereign will be ordered to lie flat on the deck beside their pieces, too. I hope so, for their sake. That is the best way to avoid injury when you have no chance to return fire. Flying splinters can be deadly.*

He glanced over his shoulder just as the French opened fire with a *second* broadside. Behind him, he heard the reassuring measured tread of Nelson pacing the Quarterdeck, accompanied by Captain Hardy, who appeared to be conversing with his Secretary John Scott. They were a pair of idiots. He heard Captain Charles Adair of the Royal Marines station his people all around the Poop. Everything was happening too quickly. Jim wished to grab his chance to save the day. In these light airs the *Victory* was moving about as fast through the water as a man might walk down Piccadilly. The *Bucentaire* was still a good mile away. She was probably firing at long range to see if she could hit the *Victory*. It was enough to drive an ambitious officer like Jim mad with feverish anticipation. When would he get his chance to strut his stuff and show the whole world how determined and how forceful a great leader he was?

Jim heard more sounds of incoming shot, and then, looking up, he saw a hole appear suddenly in the main-topgallant sail!

They have found our range. Now all hell will break loose, and we shall have no way to fire back for the next twenty minutes. Here is my chance to shine! Where is Corrie? I don't see her. What is my sister up to? I wonder why she has left the deck? Bad luck, Corrie! You missed your opportunity! Better leave it all to brother James. Grim Jim is here! The officer of the day! Here I come!

An enemy round shot struck the fore brace bitts at the base of the mainmast. Splinters flew, and Jim jumped to his feet in time to see one of the jagged bits of wood glance off Captain Hardy's shoe as the good man was pacing along the deck and chatting with his secretary. The splinter sent Hardy's shoe buckle skittering away across the deck!

Jim thought that was hilarious.

A moment later the captain's secretary John Scott was cut in two by a round shot, and his remains were sent flying.

Nelson turned to his friend Hardy. 'Is that poor Scott that is gone?'

Jim saw Hardy nod.

'Poor fellow!' said Nelson, and then continued to walk the deck as if on parade.

Jim, desperate to give an order, any old order, turned to a midshipman of nineteen, Thomas Goble, and gave Goble a fierce frown, and a jerk of the head. Obediently the brave lad darted in to take the Secretary's place at Hardy's side. Just as well, really! Hardy would need someone close at hand to take messages and to run errands. Jim began breathing heavily.

The French have found the range, From now on, their firing will be relentless.

He braced himself for his chance to win the war. In his dreams all his rival officers would be mown down, and then he alone would face the anger of the enemy, and turn the tables with his brilliant savoir faire, saying something witty and memorable that would read well in the *Morning Chronicle*.

Round after round came smashing into the *Victory*, each missive sending more jagged splinters of wood flying in all directions. Within a few short minutes, half of the ship's complement of forty Royal Marines lay wounded or killed.

Jim's mouth fell open. He gaped! So many dead! So quick!

He saw Nelson turn to the Royal Marines commander Captain Adair and heard him say 'Disperse your remaining men around the ship, captain.'

Jim caught his breath.

What was Nelson doing?

Without the marines up on the poop deck to keep an eye out for enemy sharpshooters, the danger to Lord Nelson is going to be far greater. He knows that. He is sacrificing himself! Well, I won't be sacrificing myself, not anytime soon. I need to be seen and heard giving the order that wins the battle. But what order? And when am I to give it? I had better think of something. Fast.

But Jim was finding it hard to think of anything clearly with his ship being shot to pieces all around him.

With an almighty crash an incoming roundshot shattered the ship's wheels hidden under the shelter of the jutting ledge of the Poop Deck, depriving the *Victory* of her easiest way to steer.

'Man the relieving tackles!' ordered Captain Hardy immediately, and Jim heard Tom repeat that order. He saw Tom dash below to see to it. As Tom left the deck, Jim heard Nelson say 'This is too warm work, Hardy, to last long.'

Jim nodded to himself. He had to agree. Warm work it was indeed! Poor Tom would be hard pressed to find twenty people to haul on the starboard tiller line *and* another twenty to haul on the port tiller line. Jim grinned. He rubbed his hands together. Soon his moment of glory would come. But first he had to make sure the *Victory* was steerable.

He turned to Anne's son, the junior officer on watch. 'Fraser! We need forty strapping miners from Little Sark. The strongest and biggest men and women you can find. Go find them, and tell them to report to the steering flat. Run all the way!'

Fraser Keeper parroted his orders navy-fashion and dashed off to fetch the biggest and best hands he could find. The boy seemed to have a firm grasp of the tactical situation. He was a promising young officer that one. If the lad survived this battle, then he might go far in the Navy. Not as far as Jim, of course. Jim was going to be First Lord of the Admiralty. All he had to do was keep a cool head and do something incredibly brilliant.

Jim looked about him, trying assess the damage done to the *Victory* thus far. It was pretty bad. Blood and bodies everywhere.

If coaxed, the women and men from Little Sark detailed for the steering flat would obey Tom's orders to pull one line or the other to shift the *Victory*'s huge tiller the moment a steering order was given. The *Victory* would have to be swung around to engage the enemy and open fire. For the time being she was being pounded to bits while unable to retaliate. If this was Nelson's plan, it was pitiful. Jim would do better. He'd teach them all how to win a battle. He'd teach them not to turn down his requests for independent command. He'd see about *that. Today.*

He had sent young Fraser dashing below in search of the biggest, brawniest hands he could find to man the tiller lines.

Would Fraser find them?

6

CHAPTER

FRASER WAS SMART.

His mother had explained Nelson's plan to pass under the stern of the *Santissima Trinidad*, ahead of Villeneuve's flagship the *Bucentaure*, and then rake both ships in passing, but Fraser could see with his own eyes that that plan would not work now that the ship's wheels had been smashed to bits, and there was no sea room left to squeeze through the French line as planned. Nelson might have to settle for the lesser option of opening fire on the stern of the *Bucentaure* instead.

If that were the case, then Fraser had only minutes in which to find some big, burly women and men to tail onto those tiller lines. His thoughts were clear.

The sooner Nelson gives that helm order, the better for us all. We are being demolished! I had better hurry.

Fraser braved the open deck through a murderous hail of incoming shot from no less than five enemy vessels, one of them being the vast and cumbersome *Santissima Trinidad*. By the time he reached the companionway, he was amazed to find himself peppered from head to toe by flying splinters. He heard Corrie's brother Jim, hatless, shout an order to his gun crews to jump to their feet and double-shot their guns. Fraser whistled. Things must be growing serious.

Then Fraser heard Captain Hardy, bewildered by the intense bombardment, turn to Admiral Nelson and ask 'Which of the enemy shall we engage?'

To this question Nelson replied 'I cannot help it. Go on board where you please. Take your choice!'

Fraser heard no more as he dived below in his search for the women and men from Sark. He knew that any helm order given at this critical moment could not be obeyed without at least *forty strong men and women* in the tiller flat to tail onto the tiller lines and move the Victory's gigantic rudder and steer the ship.

He slid down the steps navy-fashion, dashed past the crews in the lower gun deck and burst into the Mess.

He breathed a sigh of relief. Here were the very folk he needed! He rattled off the names of the dozen largest and toughest miners of Sark.

'Follow me! On the double!' he cried and then led the miners racing to the steering flat.

He saluted Lieutenant Tom Potts. 'Hands to work the tiller lines, sir.'

'Well done, Mr. Keeper! Mollet, Remfrey, you and your friends are to take up the slack on this line but don't haul until I tell you. Le Feuve, Bisson, Le Maistre, and company, I want you to tag onto the other line, same story. When the order to move the rudder comes, that order will be shouted down to us through that big hole in the deckhead where the ship's wheels used to be.' He gestured upward with his thumb. 'Be ready. Be steady…'

The order came.

'Hard-a-starboard!' was shouted from the deck above.

'Hard-a-starboard it is!' bellowed Tom in reply, and then Fraser saw him nod to Le Feuve, Bisson, Le Maistre and their friends to tail onto their line and heave for all they were worth.

'Heave!' Tom shouted.

'Heave!' shrilled young Fraser, his voice high-pitched with excitement.

The brawny miners hauled away with a will, and very slowly the massive tiller swung to port, sending the mighty rudder of the *Victory*, four decks high and attached to the stern post by seven hinges, swinging to starboard to drive the *Victory* around under the stern of the *Bucentaire*. Tom Potts and Fraser Keeper exchanged looks of apprehension as the two huge warships scraped against one another with a squeal of mistreated woodwork. Talk about point-blank range! Both ships were touching one another!

Then Fraser saw the looks of dismay on the faces of the French officers who were about to be fired upon, and he felt deeply sorry for them. What was it like to look death in the face? There was no way The French could fire back. The stern of their ship was vulnerable.

War is never fair.

There was an almighty bang as the *Victory*'s forecastle smasher carronade delivered at close range a 68-pound shot topped up with five hundred musket balls.

Fraser gasped as he saw the stern windows of the enemy flag-ship implode, sending shards of glass flying.

He heard Corrie's brother Jim shout 'Fire when your guns bear!'

The deck heaved beneath his feet as the *Victory*'s guns fired on the French. The *Victory* had raked her enemy from stern to stem and now she was continuing the pounding piece by piece.

A foul smoke arose, blackening the port gun ports, and making the women and men manning the *Victory*'s guns cough and splutter.

Fraser himself could not stop coughing.

He glanced at Tom Potts and wondered why Tom was peering so intensely into the fumes.

CHAPTER

TOM HAD SEEN Captain Jean-Jacques Magendie, the commander of the *Bucentaire*, stumble and fall to the deck. Tom had met Magendie once at a meeting of natural philosophers during the Peace. He had rather liked the man. What a waste of a fine mind!

Taking a quick breath, Tom felt the smoke draw the phlogiston from inside his body. So much for Lavoisier's belief that there was a mysterious substance in the air that fed flames. Yet, you never could be sure. Lavoisier might be proved right one day. Certainly the matter was one to be decided by experiment.

'On your feet! More charges for those guns!'

Boys and girls raced to the ready hanging magazines to fetch the stitched bags filled with measures of gunpowder doled by Perowne from the powder trough in the Grand Magazine Filling Room.

On their way back, Tom saw one child killed and another perish when a ball struck the bag of powder she was holding in her arms. It was horrible. Tom bit his lip. He thought of his own little one down in the Cable Tier, and tears came to his eyes. He wondered if little Nathaniel was finding the din of the engagement upsetting.

8

CHAPTER

NATHANIEL, bedded down amid the Victory's seven mighty anchor cables coiled in the *Victory's* Cable Tier, was doing his best to make sense of what he was hearing. He knew how to use the flap of skin in the front of his head to make noises. Where were all the big people? He decided to make some noises himself in an effort to find out.

Nobody answered his cries.

He fell silent.

His world shook. Something made a very loud bang. The snaky things trembled.

He decided once again to make the big person come back. He liked the big person. The big person smelled of peas and of oatmeal.

'Waaa!' he broadcast.

There was no answer. No big person.

Wiggly things appeared near his blinking things. He heard bangs and thumps, followed by footsteps.

Ah! Big person footsteps.

Somebody was coming, after all. Good! His flap was working. His cries had been heard.

Wait! Something was wrong. No smell of peas. No smell of oatmeal.

Mama?

No smell of milk. Not Mama, then. A stranger?

Scary!

Play dead. No kicking. No waving arms. Freeze.

Big person coming nearer.

Big person breathing.

Big person smells of garlic?

Keep very, very still.

Ouch! Big person grabs arm, snatches him from sleeping place.

Danger!

Garlic Face in a hurry.

Smoke. Try to breathe. Choke.

Garlic Face trip over something.

Kick feet! Make BIG NOISE to frighten Garlic Face.

Garlic Face carrying me.

Bright light.

Crash! Crash! Crash!

Higher and higher.

Mama! Papa! Help!

9

CHAPTER

WHEN HARBOTTLE returned to the Cable Tier with his bottle of goat's milk, drawn that morning from the ship's goat that had been dumped overboard and left to drown, he found Nathaniel missing from his cradle. Harbottle's jaw dropped. He looked about frantically.

Where could the three-year-old have got to? What had become of him?

Still clutching the bottle of milk, Harbottle scrambled up the special stair that Nelson had ordered built to make it easier for him to reach the Quarter Deck while using only one arm. Harbottle paused for breath at the top of the stair. His years were catching up with him. He was loathe to tell someone that the three-year-old was missing, and that *Nathaniel had not taken his monkey*. The child loved that monkey. Harbottle had made the stuffed monkey for him, with the approval of the child's father, Lieutenant Potts, who had shown him a sketch of a real monkey he had made in the Province of Wellesley on the far side of the world.

Nathaniel would not have left that monkey behind on purpose. Harbottle suspected foul play. He feared that somebody had *stolen* Nathaniel.

He was right.

Harbottle stepped out onto the deck and bit his lip. The dead, thrown back as they fell, lay in heaps, and the shot, passing through them, had mangled them most frightfully. Several had lost their heads. Brains were splattered everywhere.

Doing his best to ignore these heaped up horrors, Harbottle approached Nathaniel's grandfather. He doffed his cap respectfully amid the clash and smash of the battle.

'Yes, Harbottle?' said Lieutenant Harriman, a little surprised to see him. 'What is the matter?'

'The little tyke is gone sir. I had him bedded down and I was off fetching his milk for him, and now he's gone, and his monkey is left behind in his crib. Somebody's snatched him, sir.'

'Are you speaking of young Nathaniel?'

'Aye, sir. Somebody must have spirited the lad away. I don't know what for, sir.' Harbottle wiped a tear from his cheek.

'Easy, now, Harbottle! Steady on! You go back down below to the Cable Tier and look after the other youngsters. Don't worry! I'll find out what has happened to Nathaniel, I promise.'

Harbottle wiped away his tears with an old kerchief that had seen better days. 'You got to find him sir.'

'I shall, Harbottle. Off you go now. Keep your head down'

Harbottle barely made it back in one piece to Nelson's stair, through heavy musket fire. He wondered what Lieutenant Harriman would do about his missing grandson.

The enemy fire grew more and more intense. The *Victory* was being shot to pieces. His ears were ringing.

He heard somebody shouting in what might be French. Harbottle frowned. The only language he knew was English.

'*Vive l'empereur! Vive l'amiral!*'

Halfway down Nelson's stair, Harbottle was knocked clean off his feet when an enemy roundshot destroyed half the steps and sent him flying.

He flew through the air. The jar of goat's milk fell from his hand and rolled away across the deck, spilling its contents.

What a waste!

Then there was a tremendous rolling rumble of guns going off one after another.

A broadside!

10

CHAPTER

'WHAT AM I HEARING?' asked Anne, her head swimming. The poison from the enemy pigeon was affecting her quite badly now. It was growing harder for her to grasp what was going on.

Corrie brought her up to date. 'The *Redoubtable* is firing at us. Boarding parties have mustered by her taffrail. Five enemy ships are bombarding us simultaneously, among them the *Bucentaure*, the *Santissima Trinidad*, and the *Redoutable*. We are hard pressed. Enemy soldiers are firing down at us from the tops. I fear for Nelson.'

'They had better not hit Admiral Nelson,' said Anne fiercely, grabbing at the standing rigging to keep herself from stumbling.

Corrie took her friend by her arm. 'At least we are keeping up our rate of fire. We, too, must doing damage. We are! See there! The main and mizzen masts of the Bucentaure are coming down. And if I'm not mistaken, the crew of the French flagship are in a panic. Look! They are trying to launch Villeneuve's barge.'

'Will they succeed?'

'No. The barge is riddled with shot. Now the barge is sinking. The French admiral won't be able to transfer his flag.'

Anne peered this way and that through the smoke. 'Any sign of our traitor?'

'Yes.' Corrie pointed. 'That's him, climbing the standing rigging! See there! He has stolen that long barrelled musket he's holding, probably from one of the fallen Marines. Wait! That's odd. He has a *child* with him. I have a bad feeling about this.'

'You had better go up after him, Corrie. I'm no good to you like this. I can't even see where I'm going,' said Anne, and swore an oath under her breath.

'I'd better have a word with my brother first,' said Corrie.

She raced along the Upper Gun Deck in search of Jim. The deck was furrowed by shot. She slipped. She skidded to a halt.

'Jim. Listen! If anything happens to Nelson, and if Hardy leaves the deck to attend to Nelson, I have promised to take Nelson's place and summon the reserves, but only if and when they are needed. The signal to call in those reserves is Number 16. Right now I have to chase down a spy who is planning to shoot Nelson in the back. Remember! If Nelson falls, it will be up to you to win the battle. Repeat my order!'

'If you can't keep your promise to Nelson, I am to keep it for you.' Jim grinned. It was *just* what he wanted. With Corrie out of the way, he, Jim, could step in and save the day!

'That's right,' said Corrie, and clapped her brother on his shoulder.

She leaped back as Lieutenant Roteley came charging along the deck with twenty-five men stolen from the great guns to join Captain Adair's squad of whom only ten brave souls were still on their feet and firing their muskets at the enemy.

The red-coated and bewigged Captain Adair saw these rein-forcements arriving. He lifted his head and bellowed an order in a voice accustomed to the din of battle.

'Roteley! Fire away as fast as you can!'

These words were barely out of Adair's mouth before a ball struck the poor man in the back of his neck, killing him outright.

Corrie's thoughts lurched as she saw him fall.

Just like that, the Victory *has lost a valuable Captain of Marines. This makes my task of stopping the spy Dupont twice as difficult. There is something oddly familiar about the child Dupont has carried up into the rigging. Why has Dupont brought a child with him on his murderous mission? Whose child is it?*

A dreadful suspicion formed in Corrie's mind.

She heard a cry from far above, and her worst fear was confirmed.

'Mama!' shouted Nathaniel.

Dear God! It is my *child. The spy has grabbed my three-year-old as a hostage.*

Furious, Corrie sprang for the mainmast shrouds. The stays were half shredded by shot and dangerous to climb. That did not stop her, not for one moment. Her ears sang. She smelled blood and vomit. Battle raged all around her. Her throat felt dry as she raced up into the tops to save her little son.

'How's it going, Billy?' she shouted to the Captain of the Maintop. 'I see half of your platform has been ripped away!'

'The duppies are in one big mash-up,' Billy Brown hollered back, and grinned, her white teeth lighting up her Jamaican face. She pointed down at the deck below. 'Dat Nelson one cool fellow.'

Corrie risked a quick glance below to see what Billy was talking about.

As if entirely unaware of the appalling slaughter going on all around him, Admiral Nelson was walking calmly with Captain Hardy, continuing to pace back and forth in the middle of the quarterdeck, putting on a show of imperturbability to encourage all of the children, women and men of the *Victory* who were still on their feet to continue resisting the French and Spanish. They simply had to go on fighting. Nelson and Hardy themselves were doing their level best to ignore the flying splinters and the crashing guns. Both seemed to be living charmed lives.

Corrie sought her quarry.

'Have you seen Seaman Dupont, Billy? He has grabbed my child. I think he's up to no good,' she said, peering up into the heights of the rigging through the swirling gun smoke.

'Dat one? Yes, I see him. Dat one up to no good. Dat one heading for the tops wid a long barrel. Dat one got your pickney.'

'I know. Where is he now?'

'There!' Billy pointed. 'Him in standing rigging. Yuh no seet?'

'Yes, I see him. He is planning to shoot Nelson, and using my child for cover. We have to stop him. Come with me, Billy. We'll do this together.'

'I is right behind you.'

Corrie went up the shrouds hand over hand as fast as fire. She did not look behind her. Her eyes were fixed on the spy Dupont and her little boy.

I see the villain clearly now, up ahead of me. What is he doing with my youngster? He has snatched my baby out of the safety of the Cable Tier. He has yanked my child up here, exposing him to this merciless hail of ball and shot, but to what end? Does he hope to prevent me from intervening to prevent an assassination? You bet I'm going to intervene. I can't let that bastard shoot Nelson. I just hope I'm not too late. Hello, what's this? Dupont is wrapping his legs around a stay. He has my Nathaniel under one arm. He is holding that purloined musket in his other arm. Oh my Lord! He is taking aim at Nelson with one arm while holding Nathaniel with the other.

'Kick, Nathaniel! Squirm! That's it! Keep on kicking! Do your best to spoil his aim. I'm coming for you!'

Heaven help us! What if Dupont shoots Nelson in the back? Dupont hasn't fired yet. Perhaps the powder smoke is too thick for him to get a clear shot. I think that must be the case. He is waiting for the smoke to clear. I bet he is wondering why the ready hanging magazines have not exploded!

'Keep on kicking, Nathaniel! Keep on squirming! Stop that bastard from taking aim! Mama is coming!'

Corrie's heart rate increased. The roar of the battle receded and ballooned. It was hard to keep her footing in these damnable ripped up shrouds. Her hands shook. She was outraged. The smoky fog of war swirled around her. For a moment she thought she saw some of Billy's Dutty Duppies making fun of her, their ghastly faces swimming in and out of focus as they fed on her fear.

She pulled herself together.

She had no time for Billy's Dutty Duppies.

I have to bring Dupont down before the smoke clears. Sorry, Nathaniel. I'm going to have to risk your life if I am to save Nelson.

She grabbed a frayed footrope with her left hand, gave the hank a yank to make sure that it was sound, and then kicked off from the ripped rigging and swung through the air, her heavy uniform jacket ballooning behind her. A rush of cold air smashed into her face. She skimmed over the heads of Billy Brown's people. She felt half human and half hawk. All of England looked to Nelson for victory, and this child-snatching spy dared to use *her baby* as cover while he shot England's greatest sailor in the back? There was no way she could allow *that*!

'Think again, Monsieur Dupont!'

I shall put an end to your mischief. I shall deal you a blow from which you shall never recover. Whatever happens, Dupont, you are going to die. I'm not going to let you shoot the greatest admiral in the Royal Navy in the middle of the most important naval action of his entire career. I'm coming for you, Dupont!

Aha! Dupont has seen me. He has heard me shouting.

I am shouting at him and he is shouting something back at me.

She hit the beat-up remains of the crow's nest feet-first, doing her best to keep her balance more than two hundred feet up in the air.

If I fall from this height, I shall die. So be it. I'll take him with me.

Corrie swung herself around and brought her pistol to bear. She saw Nathaniel's white face. Her little boy looked so frightened. That made her hopping mad. How *dare* Dupont use a child as a shield? *Her* child?

At that moment the *Santissima Trinidad* fired a devastating broadside, and then, a moment later, Captain Lucas's 74 *Redoutable* raked the *Victory*'s decks.

A quick glance down at the *Redoutable*'s deck told Corrie the dreadful story. She saw the enemy commander Lucas pacing his quarterdeck. She heard Lucas shout an order. The mast to which she was clinging shuddered as the *Redoutable*'s broadside shattered several of the *Victory*'s gun ports, knocking one 12-pounder clean off its gun carriage and sending the members of the gun crews flying through the air. It was heart-breaking to see. The tiny platform on which Corrie was trying to keep her balance cracked, splintered, and then gave way beneath her.

Dupont took careful aim at Nelson. At this close range, Dupont could not possibly miss. There was only one thing Corrie could think of that might stop him. She was the only person in a position to bring the spy down. But at what cost? At the cost of her child.

'I'm sorry, Nathaniel,' she said, choking. 'I'm sorry.'

She took aim at Dupont's chest.

She pulled the trigger.

Dupont screamed. He let go of Nathaniel. He lurched sideways. The weight of his body pinned Corrie to the mast.

'Nathaniel!' cried Corrie, lunging desperately to save her son.

But she missed the child's outstretched hand by inches.

She glimpsed the startled look on Nathaniel's face as the three-year-old began his long fall down to the deck.

My baby is gone.

With his last gasp, this treacherous Dupont has pinned me to the mast. I can smell his garlic breath. He is dying but he seems determined to take me with him.

'Not on my watch, Dupont!' she yelled in his face.

She played her trump card.

She stamped as hard as she could on the remaining broken boards.

The crow's nest collapsed, sending both Corrie and Dupont tumbling through the air to certain death.

Corrie's last thought was 'I should have been a better mother.'

11

CHAPTER

CORRIE'S BROTHER JIM, stunned and disoriented by the smashing attack from the *Redoutable*, scrambled across the splintered wreckage of the ship's wheels. Bleeding from numerous abrasions, he managed to regain the Quarter Deck. He looked about him in an effort to assess the progress of the battle as a whole. It was hard to see through all the smoke and flames, but Nelson's plan seemed to be working more or less. Both flagships, that of Nelson and that of Collingwood, had succeeded in breaking through the Spanish and French lines. Both were now surrounded by enemy vessels, but Jim was glad to see that those enemy vessels were themselves having to ward off bombardment after bombardment from one English ship of the line after another. Jim was dazed and unsure of himself. The thunder of the guns and the cries of despair from the wounded would stay with him for the rest of his life. Corrie had told him of her private conversation with Nelson. Perhaps this was the moment at which Nelson would decide to summon the smaller and faster ships he had placed in reserve? He looked about for Corrie. Where was she? Strange that she was not on the Quarter Deck. She had said something about chasing a spy.

The deck was strewn with wounded and the remains of those who had died. Jim was glad that Vice-Admiral Nelson had not been hurt. The decision to call in the fleet reserves lay with Nelson for as long as he remained alive and was able to give orders.

Jim stared in awe at the Admiral, still walking the deck as if in utter disregard of the dangers of incoming fire from all five enemy ships now surrounding the *Victory*. He saw Captain Hardy leave Nelson's side for a few moments. He heard Hardy shout an order down through the gaping hole where the ship's wheels had been. He heard several burly miners from Sark shout encouragement to one another as they strained at the tiller lines to move the ship's vast rudder.

He watched Hardy hurry back and rejoin the pacing Nelson.

He saw the pair of senior officers turn on their heels together near the smashed hatchway, in order to resume their solemn walk side by side amid all these unspeakable horrors.

A musket was fired from *Redoutable* by a French marksman abaft and below the *Victory*'s mizzen-top. The enemy marksman was fifteen yards from Nelson. The marksman might easily miss, for muskets were far from reliable.

But the Frenchman did not miss.

The ball struck the epaulette on Nelson's left shoulder.

Jim saw Nelson fall with his face on the deck. He saw Captain Hardy spin on his heel, aghast at the sight of Nelson lying there. Jim watched with his heart in his mouth as Marine Sergeant Secker and two seamen ran to help the admiral back on his feet.

For the second time, Jim looked about for his sister Corrie. Where was she? Before the battle his sister had promised the admiral that she would act promptly were the admiral wounded.

Now the admiral was wounded. People were dashing to Nelson's side. The great man was unable to regain his feet, even with assistance. Jim's heart sank. The wounded admiral would have to be carried below to the Orlop Deck. The people of the fleet would lose heart if they came to know that Nelson was hurt. Better the fleet be left in ignorance for the time being.

Jim stared at Nelson, hoping the great man would say something brave and funny and make light of his injury, as he had done in the past.

'Can you stand?' asked Hardy.

He and the Admiral were fast friends.

Nelson's reply was terse and to the point. 'They have done for me at last, Hardy.'

'I hope not,' replied Hardy, deeply shocked.

'Yes, my backbone is shot through.'

Jim saw a tear roll down Hardy's cheek.

Nelson turned his head. Was he looking for Corrie? Was he hoping to remind Jim's sister with a meaningful glance of that private conversation he had had with her just before the battle?

It was just as well that Corrie had told Jim about that conversation.

Were he to fall, Nelson had told her, and if Harvey left the Quarter Deck, then it would be up to her, Corrie, to bring the battle to a successful conclusion.

Jim paced back and forth, thinking hard. The other ships in the fleet did not yet know that Nelson had been wounded. Corrie was not here to do as she had promised. Nelson could see no sign of her. Nor could Jim. Now that Nelson had been hit, the admiral needed to be sure that Corrie was alive and ready to obey his secret instructions, for Corrie had an instinctive grasp of the tactical situation. Nelson's eye now lit on Jim. Nelson raised an eyebrow questioningly.

Jim nodded curtly to let the admiral know that he was privy to what the admiral had ordered Corrie to do.

The distraught Hardy tried to pull himself together. 'Carry the admiral to the cockpit,' he said hoarsely.

Two burly seamen carried the admiral carefully down the ladder to the Middle Gun Deck,

As he was being carried off, Nelson beckoned to a young officer.

'My Lord?' said the youngster, awed.

'New tiller lines are needed. They are to be rove at once.'

'New tiller lines to be rove. Aye, aye, admiral.'

'There is a handkerchief in my pocket. Cover my face with it. I wish to be unnoticed by the crew.'

'I'm sorry you are hurt, sir,' said the young officer, and did as he was told. 'Lieutenant Ram, has been killed, and so has Mr. Whipple,' the youngster added for no particular reason, his voice shaky. He sounded lost, bewildered. Things were happening so *fast*.

'Deliver my message!' said the admiral sharply, his voice muffled by the handkerchief.

'Yes, sir,' said the young man. He saluted the fallen admiral and darted up the ladder to pass the word about the tiller lines to Captain Hardy.

He found Hardy standing stock still on the quarterdeck, dazed and upset.

He listened to the message.

'Tiller lines?' Hardly said, puzzled. 'Are you sure he said tiller lines?'

'Yes, sir. Admiral's orders, sir.'

'We had better see to the matter then. Come with me. The deck is yours, Lieutenant Harriman,' said Hardy, and the distraught captain left the quarterdeck in a hurry, bound for the steering flat.

Jim's brain shifted gears. There was nothing wrong with the tiller lines. He had inspected them himself.

This is a ruse by Nelson. He wants Hardy to leave the deck, so Corrie can take over and obey his secret instructions. But Corrie is not here to do that, so I had better do it for her. This is my chance to keep her promise to Nelson and win the war at sea. For a few precious minutes I, Captain James Harriman, am in command of the greatest warship ever built at Chatham, in the middle of what may turn out to be the most decisive naval battle ever fought by the Royal Navy. I must think like Corrie. I must act like Corrie.

It was a sobering moment for Jim.

His thoughts crystallized.

What would Corrie do? The Fleet has no idea that Nelson is no longer in charge. Any orders given from the Victory *will be assumed to come from Nelson. So I must* be *Nelson, heart and soul. I must think like Nelson. I must send the very signal Nelson would send were he still on his feet. What would Corrie were she here to keep her promise?*

She would call in the reserve. I am sure she would.

He knew Nelson's reserve vessels were all fast sailors, crammed with fighting hands. They were awaiting an order from Collingwood or from Nelson to join in the battle and engage the enemy. Nelson had told Corrie in confidence that the secret signal inviting that reserve squadron to join the fray was Signal Number Sixteen in the signals book. That was a signal consisting of two flags. The signalman would know which ones.

Jim couldn't wait. He was so excited. He was going to win the oceans for England. He turned to his father and said gleefully 'Lieutenant Harriman. Make a signal to the fleet. Signal Number Sixteen.'

'Signal Number Sixteen. Aye, aye, captain.' His father spun on his heel and bellowed at the Yeoman of Signals. 'Number Sixteen. Jump to it, Eaves.'

'Aye, aye, sir,' said the Yeoman, and within minutes, three pairs of flags ordering Nelson's reserve to join the battle were flying from the three mastheads of the *Victory*.

'Execute.'

Down came the flags. The moment the flags came down, the order would be obeyed. Jim hoped that someone in the reserve squadron had seen the signal through the choking fumes and roiling clouds of smoke.

The foretop lookout shouted down to say that the reserve squadron was making sail.

'They must have had their glasses trained on us, and their hands waiting out on the yards, poised for the go-ahead,' said Archibald Harriman, who had returned from the defeated *Santissima Trinidad* just in time to give Jim an encouraging grin. He had never been prouder of his son than at this moment.

Jim nodded, but he had his reservations.

He had just played England's last card.

We had better win. I have just thrown in our reserves. I shall have to live with the consequences of what I have just done for the rest of my life. I think I have done what Corrie would have wanted were she here in my place. But I find her absence disturbing. I hope nothing has happened to her. I wish she were hear to see my hour of glory. I'd show her a thing or two.

As for keeping the wounding of Nelson a secret, what with all the smoke and the noise of battle, that was easy enough for now. Few indeed in the *Victory* knew that Nelson had been hit. Nelson had been carried below down into the shadowy world of the Orlop Deck, but he was still alive. The admiral was still in command for as long as he was able to whisper orders.

Jim heard someone curse. Turning on his heel, she saw the nineteen-year-old midshipman John Pollard up on the poop deck, a long gun to his shoulder. Young Pollard had seen Nelson brought down by an enemy sharpshooter, and tears were streaming down his cheeks. He was firing shot after shot, trying to bring down the enemy marksman responsible for wounding Nelson. Jim saw Quartermaster King come to Pollard's assistance. He handed the young officer a parcel of ball-cartridge, but then, a moment later. the Quartermaster himself was brought down by that very marksmen in the *Redoutable* at whom Pollard was firing so assiduously.

Jim shook his head.

Is that what has happened to my sister? Has she, too, been shot by some French marksman? This could be the turning point of my career. If I play my cards right.

The French are boarding us from the Redoutable. *Here come four enemy boarders dashing across their fallen mainyard which they are using as a handy bridge from their vessel to ours. Well! I can do something about* that.

He grabbed up a cutlass lying on the deck and ran to deal with the enemy boarders.

He was halfway across the deck when the French had the audacity to fire *upwards* through the *Victory*'s deck. Splinters flew everywhere. Lieutenant Ram went down, his legs shot away from under him.

Jim waved his cutlass. 'Ingham! Lyons! Lieutenant Ram is injured. Carry him below to Dr. Beatty.'

Jim sprang onto the toppled mainyard, pushed one enemy overboard and never even heard the splash as the fellow hit the sea. Then he grappled with a second, while shouting over his shoulder an order to the men and women manning the relieving tackle down in the steering flat. 'Hard to port, Dutty Boukman!' he yelled.

Boukman acknowledged the order with a wave, and, moments later, the huge rudder began to swing.

The gap between the *Victory* and the *Redoutable* widened, sending the *Redoutable*'s fallen mainyard plunging into the ocean, carrying several more boarders with it.

For good measure Jim shoved another assailant over the rail. He raced back across the quarterdeck, the din of battle all around him. It was as well that Nelson's reserve ships were speedy and easy to sail. Hopefully they would come to the *Victory*'s rescue soon. They had better, or there would be little left to save.

The battle had to be reaching a climax. Success or defeat? With the fall of Nelson, defeat seemed the most likely prospect.

Suddenly a thunderous explosion jarred the air as a nearby ship blew up. Flaming debris rained down all around him. For a few frightening moments Jim found it hard to breathe.

The blast of hot air that accompanied the explosion sent the mizzen-mast of the *Victory*, shot though earlier, crashing down in ruin. The tumbled rigging swept Jim clean off his feet.

12

CHAPTER

CORRIE'S FATHER, Lieutenant Archibald Harriman, took a running jump and landed on all fours on the shattered deck of the *Santissima Trinidad*. She was a living hell. Shot after shot had torn the sails to ribbons. It was as if the canvas had been clawed by a Roc. Spars had been turned to splinters and thick cables of hemp sheared through as if by a monstrous scythe. Rivulets of blood ran all over the deck, making strange patterns as the great ship rolled helplessly with the swells, tipping this way and that. A Spanish officer had hung a large British Union flag over the side as a token of surrender.

It was time to take charge and give orders. 'Round up the prisoners! Stretcher party over here. This fellow is wounded. Gently with him. Take him back to the ship. Maybe Beatty can save his leg.'

But where was his daughter

'Corrie!' he hollered. 'Corrie, are you there?'

No answer.

He burst into the captain's cabin. He snatched up the logbook and signals manual. You never knew what might be useful in time of war. Somebody at the Admiralty would know what to do with the *Santissima Trinidad*'s books.

Here was a junior officer offering his reversed sword as a token of surrender. His elders must have been cut down by the *Victory*'s barrage. The fellow looked upset. A Spanish senorita stared at him, fury and anguish written across her face. Suddenly she whipped a knife out from under her bodice and, shouting something defiant in his face, she lunged at him.

13

CHAPTER

AS CORRIE FELL from the towering height of the shattered crow's nest, she was pleased to have given up her life to bring down that wretched spy Dupont who had dared to infiltrate her crew. Dupont would have shot Nelson in the back had she not intervene. So it was her life for Nelson's life. Ever since the Battle for Copenhagen she had considered Nelson a friend as well as her superior officer.

Faster and faster she fell. Her last moments on Earth seemed to expand. Every detail of the ship's rigging came to her attention. With an unearthly crystal clarity her eye noted that the backstay travellers used for hoisting the topgallant yards had jammed in the hoops used to secure the topsail to the topmast. What a tangle! Only in battle could such a muddle go unattended. The topsail had sagged into a giant's hammock.

Moments later she hit the giant's hammock. The blow winded her but did not kill her.

Her fall broken, she began to slide helplessly from reef-band to reef-band.

She saw the edge of the sail come rushing towards her.

She made a grab for the running rigging. She missed.

She was catapulted out over the ocean.

Better to hit water than the deck, she thought.

I don't know how to swim.

She crashed into the sea.

From her very earliest days she had feared Water. Water was her nemesis.

Now Water was here. Water had finally caught up with her.

Hitting the sagging topsail had knocked the breath out of her lungs.

Like many of her crew, she had never learned to swim.

She could not even breathe!

Her thoughts were desperate.

I hear a deep reverberating thunder! A mighty roar in my ears!

I am no more, I find myself in that strange half-seen world Tom stumbled into years ago when he was thrown down upon the deck and rendered unconscious.

I see an altar wrought in stone and bone.

Nathaniel? Are you here?

I am so sorry for my crew.

I am so sorry for my lover, my brother, my patient father and my faraway mother.

Boom boom, boom says my heart.

It must be over.

The whole thing must be over. Goodbye, Life!

Somewhere far away I imagine the rising sun is lighting up the dark clouds of dawn, and the crescent moon. I remember the taste of mango in the Province of Wellesley! So many wonders! But all those gorgeous treats are sliding away from me now, for I shall not see, hear or touch the like again.

All those echoes, all those flavours, all those moments of joy and discovery, sadness and reparation, are heading back into the deeps from which I suppose they came, that treacherous sea that gives birth to us, nurtures us and gobbles us up!

When I was young and the water closed over my head I was frightened and furious, but I was curious too. I think I was alarmed that this was all there was, that this was all I would know, that this was all that I would ever truly grasp.

Now that I am grown, now I give the orders I once obeyed, and now that I have fallen, and my child is dead, my ancient enemy has me by the throat, and I have to ask: What was it all about?

Was it about love?

I should have been a better mother.

A stark, bewildering feeling was overcoming her by degrees as her thoughts waned. Ghastly flashes of blood-red light intimated something coming, something tremendous, forking flames of otherness, wrapped in darkness. The Wetness that had tried to kill her when was very young had found her at last. Bereft of her child, she lacked the will to live again.

That imploring look in Nathaniel's eyes was seared into her memory. Better to die here, out of sight, beneath the waves in this half-world. Here was a fitting end for Corrie Harriman.

Her epitaph would be:

Drowned at sea.

14
CHAPTER

THE *Téméraire* appeared out of the smoke, breaking through the enemy line astern of the *Redoutable*. Captain Harvey opened fire with his heavy guns, bringing down the *Redoutable*'s upper masts, sails and rigging, and killing two hundred brave French women, men and children.

For a moment Captain Harvey, watching the appalling slaughter, feared that the hail of shot might pass clear through the enemy ship and smash into the *Victory*, but that did not happen.

He wiped his brow. He looked about him.

He shouted to Captain Lucas of the *Redoutable* to surrender and not prolong what was a hopeless resistance, but the only reply he got was another angry volley. The barrage resumed. The *Redoutable*'s mainmast came crashing down in ruin, and, a few moments later, her stern burst into flames.

Nelson's friend and fellow officer Captain Hardy returned in a hurry to the Quarter Deck of the *Victory*, having found nothing amiss with the tiller lines, and looked about him, puzzled. He felt very strongly that he should go below and have another word with Nelson. His friend was *dying*.

'Keep an eye on things here, Lieutenant Harriman. Have our fire fighters douse that blaze.'

'Aye aye, captain.'

Hardy vanished back down below, anxious to see how Nelson was doing.

15

CHAPTER

NORAH STEWART, once the Ship's Laundress in the *Swift*, but now the Ship's Cook in the *Victory*, had a free run of the galley. She was proud of her galley. The *Victory*'s galley boasted an eight-foot-high iron fire hearth with this tremendous cooking range, topped by a copper chimney. Two vast copper kettles were used to prepare soup for eight hundred children, women and men. Both kettles had been thoroughly scoured before the battle. Each kettle was six feet high and four and a half feet wide. Since the galley stove and the kettles could not be used during the action, Norah decided that it was high time to stow her toddlers Ida and Bessie inside one of the kettles to ride out the engagement.

She went over her plan in her head.

I shall hide both my bairns together in the one kettle. That way they'll keep one another company, and won't be bawling.

So she made a game of it, laying the huge kettle on its side so the pair could crawl in and then very slowly tipping the great cauldron while talking to both youngsters cheerfully. Once the kettle was upright and both children were settled down in the bottom, she handed them two dolls sewn by the ship's witch.

The puir wee souls will need something to play with while I am away at my duty station seeing to the wounded.

Norah tiptoed out of the galley. War was a terrible thing when it parted a woman from her bairns. For how long would she be parted from these two? It was hard to say. Already the battle was louder than any engagement she had ever known. At any moment the action might take her life or her children's lives.

I hope my pair fall asleep. I hope the sounds of fighting do not give Ida and Bessie nightmares for the rest of their lives.

She returned directly to the Sickbay, where the surgeon, James Barry saw the tears in Norah's eyes and threw her a questioning look.

'I have stowed my wee ones out of harm's way inside a copper kettle in the galley,' Norah explained. 'If anything should happen to me, someone should know where to find them.' She burst into tears. 'Cheery byes, blue skies,' she said.

The Surgeon spoke to Norah in a calm voice. 'You have done well, Norah. Your children will have a good chance of surviving.' She handed the distraught mother a pile of materials. 'We'll be wanting for bandages and slings. Make as many as you can.'

'Yer a braw one, Dr. Barry,' she said. 'I hope you survive.'

'I intend to,' the Surgeon replied drily, 'for I am to train with Barber Surgeons of Edinburgh. They have offered me a place.'

'Edinburgh!' cried Norah. 'Oh, how I miss Edinburgh. Not that I saw very much of South Bridge. But my oh my! You'll be a Barber Surgeon! There are no better.'

'May I ask you to look after things here for a little while, Norah?' said the medical officer. 'Word has reached me that Nelson has been wounded, and Mr. Beatty may need an assistant. I won't be gone for long.'

Norah tut-tutted. Oh, no! Nelson hurt *again?*

The puir gadgie. He lost an eye and an arm already. Whatever has he lost this time? It beggars the imagination. And he such a fine peach of a man.

Dr. Barry had similar thoughts as she made her way to the part of the Orlop Deck where Nelson was lying. When she overheard Nelson remonstrating with his close friend Captain Hardy, her heart sank.

Death was not going to be very long in coming, apparently. She had a brief *sotto voce* exchange with her fellow surgeon Beatty. When it became clear that there was nothing she could do to help, Barry made her way sadly back to the Surgery, feeling dispirited, She was careful to say nothing of Nelson's condition to Norah. For her part, Norah was wise enough not to ask. One look at the Surgeon's face was enough.

16

CHAPTER

A SHOT struck the muzzle of the gun Jeanette was preparing to sponge out, and the force of the impact sent her sent flying straight over the side of the *Victory* and into the sea. Unlike Corrie, Jeanette had no fear of water. She had grown up on the island of Little Sark, and had had been a swimmer from an early age.

She surfaced, gasped for breath, and then cried out for help in her native tongue, the patois of Sark. Moments later she was rescued from drowning by the French-speaking crew of a guard boat, who delivered her to their own ship, the *Indomptable*. Once safely aboard the French 74, she was given her a towel to dry herself off and then, minutes later, after she had had time to pull herself together, she was put to work.

She was stationed in the passage of the fore-magazine, handing up powder. Shivering with cold, and still rubbing her wet hair, she went to work with a will. Common sense told her she dared not change her clothes for fear of being revealed a woman, but she had an odd feeling that there was something else important she had to remember, something to do with a young man of about her own age whom she was fond of? Strange that she could not recall that young man's name! Her brain was not working properly. She must have been in some kind of an explosion? Yes, her ears were still ringing. She was not even sure which side of this war she was supposed to be on.

I suppose I am lucky that I can remember my own name. Wait a minute! What is my name?

She heard shouts of panic from above, and without warning or explanation her fellow powder monkeys ran away, leaving their bags of gunpowder lying on the deck. Something bad must have happened. Wait a minute! Was that *smoke* she was smelling?

'*Aidez-moi!*'

No answer.

She abandoned her linen powder-bag and tried to find her way up to the main deck but all of the ladders leading upward had been burned away. She heard distant shouts of panic and despair. Evidently a fierce fire had started somewhere on the upper deck. Now the fire was burning downward deck by deck. The smoke was becoming darker and more choking, and Jeanette had nobody to turn to. She told herself sternly not to panic.

For a while she wandered the lower deck, bewildered, wending her way among the mangled corpses of the dead and wounded. Then, without warning, one of the great guns from the deck above fell through the burnt planks and slammed into the boards, missing her by ten feet. Far too close for comfort!

I have to escape. Perhaps I can get back into the sea?

She scrambled out of the nearest gun port, grabbed ahold of one of the ship's rudder chains, and then worked her way inch by inch to the back of the rudder.

*Soon the flames will reach the magazine. When it does, this
entire ship will blow up.*

The lead which lined the rudder trunk began to melt, and
the molten lead dripped down upon her. Owch! That really hurt!
Oh, thank you *so* much. She decided to leap back into the sea, but
then recalled her earlier experience of trying to swim in water-
logged clothes, and decided she would fare better if she got rid
of her clothes entirely. She undressed and jumped naked into the
waves. What will happen to me this time, I wonder? Join the Navy
and die a thousand deaths!

Other women and men had abandoned their ships and were
swimming about in the waves near her. One man brought her a
six-foot length of burned plank and told her to put it under her
arms. Then he supported her until a ship's boat appeared out of
the fog of war.

One of the seamen manning the boat dragged her aboard.
She was amazed. This was the second time she had been rescued
in the same day. When her rescuers saw that she was shivering
with cold and shock, *and* that she was *a young woman with no
clothes on*, they lost no time in providing her with garments. One
rower pulled off his trousers, another parted with his jacket, while
a third gave her a handkerchief to dab the wounds made by the
molten lead on her neck, shoulders and legs. The seamen were
speaking English among themselves. She recognized several faces.
Surely they were from the *Victory*?

Before she knew it, *Jeanette was back aboard her own ship*,
feeling thoroughly confused and trying to remember how she had
ever left the ship in the first place. She heard a distant a muffled
explosion amid the din of the engagement. Probably that was the

French ship she had served on so briefly that had just blown up. It was becoming harder and harder to tell one ship from another in the chaos of the battle.

A startling memory surfaced. She remembered the whine of an incoming shot, the crash as the gun was dismounted from its carriage, and the ghastly sight of her fellow gun crew being tossed into the air. She recalled hearing their cries of anguish as she herself had been sent flying , and then the stunning shock of the cold seawater.

That special young man, whose name she was still trying to recall: had he survived? She could not remember.

She stiffened.

A thought popped into her head.

I should be at my station!

She broke into a run, heading for the Upper Gun Deck. All her plagues had come in one day, so much torment and sorrow was given her and all the company in ships and sailors, and now she was running in the smoke of her own burning.

Fraser Keeper, the young man whose name had escaped Jeanette's mind, had been at his post when the shot had struck the muzzle of the gun whose crew he was supervising, killing or wounding a dozen. He had surmised that the incoming shot had been a large one, for it had split into a number of pieces, each of which had claimed a victim. He himself had received a blow to the head from which he was not sure he would recover. Something was definitely amiss with his mind. He could not even recall the name of that broad-shouldered girl from Little Sark who had been sent flying overboard.

'Lawford, help me,' he said to a fellow survivor, and together they threw the mangled body of Jack Ingham out of the stern port, his stomach having been shot away, rendering him beyond hope. The gun had been dismounted. The carriage had been badly split. The ship's fourth lieutenant, Lyons, took a quick look at the damage done to the gun and ordered him to abandon the weapon. Moments later, Lyons himself was brought down with a severe head wound.

As for Fraser, he found that he was reeling. When the order came to cease firing the starboard guns, he tried to get his bearings. There were several enemy ships firing at them. Making up his mind, Fraser dashed to help a portside gun crew answer the incoming fire from the *Santissima Trinidad*. He helped rake the enemy again and again, at a rate of fire of about a minute and half between firings. That was a swifter rate than that of the enemy gunners. Practice makes perfect. With his heart in his mouth, he saw the *Neptune* break the line and then fire a broadside into the *Santissima Trinidad* that carried away her mainmast, and shortly afterwards he saw that huge enemy vessel strike her colours amid withering fire from both the *Neptune* and the *Conqueror*.

The *Santissima Trinidad*'s tremendous fabric gave a deep roll with the swell to leeward. When she rolled back to windward, her masts went by the board and she became an unmanageable hulk. Her immense topsails had had every reef out, and the fall of the mass of spars, sails and rigging, plunging into the water before the muzzles of Fraser's gun, was a sight to remember. His head ached. He was still trying to recall the name of that young woman who had been so important to him. He had seen her vanish over the side. She had even cried out to him for help. If only he had been able to save her.

He peered over the rail, hoping to catch sight of her face among the hundreds thrashing about in the water. The heaving seas were filled with women, children and men, many of whom were holding on for dear life to fallen spars while crying out for assistance. He saw no sign of his young woman among those struggling in the water. Perhaps she had drowned? The very thought that she might have perished made him want to throw up. He wanted to see her again. He *had* to see her again. But there was a battle going on, and he had duties to perform.

Every shipmaster, and all of that company in ships, and the sailors cried out when they saw the smoke, and the voice of many waters was heard, and the heaven opened, and the rest of the dead lived not again for a thousand years.

17

CHAPTER

CORRIE HARRIMAN was furious. She *hated* the sea. The waves dashed together, piled high with scud, wrack and bobbing vials. A rising squall thrummed, forked, crackled and spat like live coals down a chimney, preventing her from regaining her ship. She heard a mighty creaking. The *Victory* was calling out to her as her ropes and yards stirred with the coming storm. Her baby had fallen from way up there in the crow's nest. Nobody could survive a fall from that height. The loss of her little one flooded her with despair. All she wanted to do was open her mouth and let the sea pour into her lungs. She was damned if she would,

Suddenly an underwater explosion flung her up, up, up until, tossed from wave to wave in a welter of spume, her body was slammed into the vast hull of the *Victory*. Stunned at being still alive and back on the surface of the sea, Corrie gulped fresh air into her starved lungs, and grabbed at the oak planking of her ship's hull, but found the *Victory*'s planks slimy and hard to grip. Luckily more than four hours of unending bombardment had left her ship trailing torn up shrouds and sodden hammocks. Corrie gave a cry of triumph as her half-frozen fingers dug into a trailing hammock. Was this her chance to regain her ship? Was this her chance to defeat her enemy and live to see another day?

Corrie dragged herself painfully out of the heaving wave as sky and sea roared and split and spat with rumbling thunder, and lit up the clouds, setting them ablaze.

A great rolling sea snatched her back from her hope of resurrection and hammered her back down into the unforgiving depths again, cheating her starving lungs of air once more.

But this time the hammock was still in her hands!

An experimental tug told her that the other end of the tangled mass of cordage was made fast, perhaps to some Lower Gun Deck stanchion?

She surfaced, took a deep breath, waited for the right moment, and then, when she felt another great rise of boiling froth and spume lift her into the air, she grabbed for the *Victory*'s side, got a good grip this time, and then hauled herself up, hand over hand, to regain the deck and do her duty.

Meanwhile Harbottle, the Captain's Steward, bemused by his recent fall on the Admiral's Stair, stumbled through the darkness of the Orlop Deck. Confused, he stopped to listen.

His Lordship the Admiral had been placed upon a bed, stripped of his clothes and covered with a sheet. Harbottle saw the Reverend Scott, who had been busy in another part of the cockpit, hurry to Nelson's side and say to the ship's Surgeon 'Alas, Beatty, how prophetic you were!' no doubt referring to some previous apprehension voiced before the battle.

At this point Harbottle heard Nelson say 'Doctor, I told you so. Doctor, I am gone.' Then, after a pause, Nelson reminded his priest and his surgeon that 'I have to leave Lady Hamilton and my adopted daughter Horatia as a legacy to my country.'

Harbottle was not sure exactly what the admiral meant by the word legacy, but he did notice that the Surgeon was nodding his head to show that *he* understood whatever it was that Nelson was asking of him.

Harbottle watched aghast as Beatty examined the admiral's wound. 'This won't hurt,' Beatty had said, 'but I must find the course of the ball. Ah! I see that it has penetrated deep into your chest and has probably lodged in your spine.

'Yes,' Nelson replied. 'I am sure my back is shot through.'

'We'll have to turn you to have a look. Ah! Nothing visible there, I'm afraid. So. Make me acquainted with your sensations, Lord Nelson. What can you feel?'

'I feel a gush of blood in my chest every minute, and I cannot feel anything at all in the lower part of my body. I'm finding it hard to breathe and my spine hurts where the ball struck. I felt it break my back.'

The Surgeon shook his head. Apparently the report of the gushing of blood, and the weakening pulse together told a sorry tale. From the medical point of view, Nelson's case was hopeless.

He heard the Surgeon say 'My Lord, unhappily for our country, nothing can be done for you.' Having said these words, the Surgeon then turned away and covered his face for a few moments, so overcome was he.

Harbottle's heart sank.

'God be praised, I have done my duty,' replied Nelson. 'What would become of poor Lady Hamilton if she knew my situation? Send for Hardy.'

Captain Hardy was Nelson's friend of ten years.

Hardy was not long in coming.

The Surgeon gave him a full report.

Nelson, looking up at their long faces, turned his head toward Hardy and said 'In a few minutes I shall be no more. Don't throw me overboard, Hardy.'

'Oh, no! Certainly not!'

'And take care of my dear Lady Hamilton, Hardy. Take care of poor Lady Hamilton. Kiss me, Hardy.'

Captain Hardy knelt down and kissed the dying Admiral's cheek. 'Fourteen French and Spanish ships have surrendered already, while no British ship has capitulated. It is resounding victory.'

Nelson nodded. 'Now I am satisfied.'

Hardy rose to his feet and stood for a few minutes in quiet contemplation before turning away.

Then Harbottle heard Hardy's footsteps as the Captain of the *Victory* left the Orlop Deck to return to his duties on the Quarter Deck. All this confusion surrounding the wounded Nelson had left Harbottle unsure of who was alive and who was dead.

He heard strange sounds of giggling coming from the ship's Galley and put his head in to investigate. He was just in time to see the Cook's two youngsters crawling out of a huge cooking pot that had been knocked over on its side by a stray shot.

'Well, well, aren't you a brave pair,' he said, and then, gathering them both into his arms, he headed for the Surgery to return the gigglers to their mother before they got into further mischief.

Not everyone had been accounted for. Harbottle wondered what had become of that young couple: Anne Keeper's boy and that brawny young woman miner from Sark. Whatever had become of Miss Muscles? In all then excitement, he had quite forgotten that young woman's name.

18

CHAPTER

JEANETTE could not remember her own name, as it happened. How much had she glorified herself and lived deliciously, and the crowds pressed about her, weeping and wailing, and twice cold waves had closed over her head, and then the smoke had choked her, and she had endured the boiling lead and the stifling fumes, and in her head her own name had left her so she no longer knew who she was or why she was here, only that there was someone somewhere waiting for her, someone who was understanding, someone whose eyes were welcoming, but who might not know her now that her poor face had been blistered by the dripping hot lead. If she found him, would he be able to tell her what her name was? Where now were the rousing tunes of the ship's marine band? Where were the trumpeters? Where were their instruments? She pushed through a crowd of despairing children, women and men, all scorched by a great heat. She heard voices crying out to her, but she was ashamed. Something had indeed befallen her. She could no more remember the young man's name than she could remember her own. This battle had been fearful beyond words. Would he even know her face, so blistered and sore? Was she still the same person she had been when growing up on the island of Little Sark? Was she still the same person the nameless young officer had rescued from the mineshaft? No. She had changed forever. This dreadful fight had changed her beyond all recognition. She would be surprised if her young man had not been changed too, whoever he was.

In the confusion of Jeanette's mind, the fellow of her dreams strode through a sea of glass mingled with fury. *She heard as it were the voice of a great multitude and she was an angel standing in the sun and cried out with a loud voice and the sea was a lake of fire.*

Fraser, was confused as she. *And the sea gave up the dead which were in it; and death and hell delivered up the dead which were in them.* In his muddled mind, the overturning of his gun and the maiming of his crew had left him shocked to the core and bereft. All about him the madness thundered on, and, strange to relate, he, too, had forgotten his own name. His former sense of the world was gone. Heaven, earth and sea had become one. In his vision of her, there was a moon under her feet and there were stars on her brow, and she was clothed in sunshine, but this vision was all he had left. This pressing crowd of anguished seamen crying out for the help he did not know how to give left him feeling bewildered and useless. He heard the wounded curse him for being on his feet and being still whole, but how whole was he? That was hard to judge. What is a man without a name? What is a man without the woman he loves? He was black with powder. His head throbbed. He pushed on through the pressing throng, trying to find a nameless woman. He had no need for the sun or the moon. He had seen her thrown overboard by the dismounting of the 12-pounder. Very likely she was lost to him for forever.

Unknowing, the pair were stumbling towards one another amid the appalling aftermath of the battle on the *Victory*'s decks, a battle now dying away after four hours of unremitting effort. Like so many others, he and she had become nameless and bereft. They had been torn apart, and might be doomed never to reunite. Hands reached out them, clawing, beseeching, angry, embittered, but blindly they thrust their shipmates aside and shouldered onward, each searching for the nameless other. When you have lost your wits and no longer know who you are or what you are about, then your only remaining hope lies in friendship. You have to find a friend. You have to find one person in all the world who can help you recall your own name, someone who can help you make sense of a world in which living creatures are created only to be forced to destroy one another if they wish to survive.

For a moment Jeanette caught a glimpse of a familiar face in the crowd. Was that *his* face? If so, would he be able to remember what her name was when she herself had forgotten what she was called? His face looked strangely swollen, blacked with powder and peppered by flying splinters. Perhaps it was not him. Perhaps her mind was shot. Yet there was something about those eyes, and those cheekbones. Yes, it might be him, but how to ask? How do you call out to someone whose name you no longer know? Now he was looking at her intensely, whoever he was. Now she could see a shocked look in his eyes. Perhaps he was horrified by the welts on her cheeks made by the drips of molten lead from the *Indomptable*. She had no trouble remembering *the name of the damned ship*. Perhaps she was too ugly for him? Perhaps she become too ugly for *anyone*. Perhaps he would not remember her *at all*. Perhaps she was drowning in the sea of life. Perhaps *he* was drowning in that same sea?

Now in truth the young man was *hoping* that here before him was the young woman he had rescued from the mine and taught to work the 12-pounder on the Upper Gun Deck, the wonderfully tough young woman from Little Sark with her fine, muscular shoulders. The thunder of the guns had taken away her name, and his own name for that matter, but behind those red welts on her cheeks, and that despairing gaze, here was *someone* he remembered.

It had to be her.

It *was* her.

Nearer and nearer they came to one another, pushing their way through the groaning, wailing seamen and marines. He could not call out to her! Her name had left him. He could not even introduce himself. He could not remember his own name. His sense of who he was had been scrambled by more who-knew-how-many hours of bombardment, his throat was dry, his sense of awareness shattered. All about him lay the wrecks of countless fighting ships and countless people. Had the Spanish capitulated? Were the French lowering their flags in recognition of defeat? Surely this awful day belonged to England. Surely the dreadful battle was over?

The nameless pair staggered to join one another.

Someone in the crowd shouted in horror as they came together.

She was hideous!

He was hideous!

He put his arms around her.

She hugged him back.

The crowd booed.

And then, just in time, he remembered. 'You're Jeanette!' he said.

Her face lit up. 'I am? But who are you? Wait! You are...Fraser.'

He was surprised. 'Yes, perhaps I am. Yes... I am Fraser.'

The pair kissed.

The crowd stamped their feet.

19

CHAPTER

'*ANCHOR*, Hardy, *anchor!*'

Captain Hardy hesitated, and then said 'I suppose, my Lord, that Admiral Collingwood will now take upon himself the direction of affairs from his own ship.'

'Not while I live, I hope, Hardy!' cried the wounded Nelson, trying without success to try to raise himself from his bed. 'No,' he added, 'do *you* anchor, Hardy.'

Captain Hardy looked perplexed, and the asked 'Shall *we* make the signal, sir?'

'Yes,' answered his Lordship energetically, 'for, if I live, I'll anchor.'

Collingwood nodded. 'Pass the word to the Officer of the Watch.'

20

CHAPTER

IN DEFIANCE of the odds, Corrie, half-drowned and soaked from head to foot by her immersion in the sea, sprang down from the rail onto the Quarter Deck in time to hear her brother telling his people to lower the signal to anchor. The idiot!

'Belay that!' Corrie shouted.

Jim was astonished. He swung around, his dream of fame shattered. 'Corrie! You are still alive!' He was bitterly disappointed.

'You can't drop anchor until you have cleared the Cable Tier. Have you forgotten who is sleeping among the coiled anchor cables?'

The blood drained from Jim's cheeks. 'Oh my God The ship's babies!'

'Pass the word for Harbottle!'

'Pass the word for the Captain's steward.'

'Harbottle to the Quarter Deck!

Harbottle arrived out of breath, wiping sweat from his brow. He looked shaken. He had been involved in several minor accidents on the way. 'Sir?

Corrie looked him in the eye. 'Mr. Harbottle! I want all the ship's babies removed immediately from the Cable Tier and made comfortable behind the canvas screen in the Gunroom. Run!'

Harbottle knuckled his forehead and left without a word, moving as fast as his old limbs would carry him.

'Report to me when you're done!' Corrie shouted after him, and Harbottle waved his arm in response to show that he had understood.

Then Corrie remembered that she had returned in time to save the ship's babies, *but she had not returned in time to save her own baby.* Her little Nathaniel had been dropped by that damnable spy from a height of some two hundred feet, and nothing in this world could have saved him.

She felt faint.

A strong hand grasped her arm under her right elbow, keeping her from falling in a swoon and disgracing herself in front of her fellow officers.

'No prob*lem*,' said Billy Brown quietly in her ear. 'I caught your pickney for you, cap'n. Dat Nathaniel he is one lucky baby. Right now he be down in cable tier, safe and sound. Don't you worry, cap'n. Harbottle will see your little one out of harm's way.'

Corrie could hardly believe her ears. 'He's safe? Nathaniel is alive? You *caught* him?'

Billy Brown nodded and grinned. 'No trouble. Dat one he is light as feather.'

Corrie gave a sigh of relief. All was right with the world after all. The reserves had been called in and soon the battle would be won. Lord Nelson and many others who were dear to her were wounded, and as for her poor *Victory*, the ship had been so heavily damaged Corrie felt she would be lucky to survive the coming storm, even if anchored. Battered old *Victory* might never make it back to Portsmouth.

But what of Nelson! Was he alive or dead? Her heart missed a beat.

She ran for the Orlop Deck.

Nelson lay there, propped up with a pillow. His eyes were closed. His breathing was labored.

Corrie knelt down beside him and spoke urgently in his ear. 'My brother and I did as you told us. We called in the reserves. 8 French and 9 Spanish ships of the line have surrendered and the *Achille* has been blown up. Not a single British ship of the line has been captured. It is a tremendous victory, my Lord. A wind is getting up. We are about to anchor as soon as we have cleared the babies out of the Cable Tier. My Lord? Can you hear me?'

Lord Nelson made no reply.

Corrie leaned forward and kissed the great man's forehead.

His Lordship said 'Who is that?'

Corrie answered 'Harriman.'

His Lordship replied 'God bless you, Harriman.'

THANK YOU SO MUCH

for reading Corries's War • Book 19 • TRAFALGAR! CORRIE
WINS THE WAR!

You may be wondering what became of the poor, battered *Victory*
after Trafalgar. After emergency repairs in Portsmouth, she returned
to Chatham Dockyard for an extensive refit. Treasured and refur-
bished often, the *Victory* has persisted to the present day, and I
paid her a visit recently at her dry dock at Portsmouth.

*Here is what the Chatham Dockyard Historical Society has to say
about the Victory's long service career:*

Named in honour of "the year of victories, 1759: Quebec,
Minden, Lagos, Quiberon Bay" she was not completed quickly, for
peace 'broke-out' in 1762 and her construction was delayed until
late 1763. She was launched 7th May 1765 at a cost of £63,176
and 3 shillings. After launch, she was laid up 'in ordinary' in
the Medway – quietly rotting for several more years before she
was brought into service in 1778 and required extensive repairs
before she was fit for her first service during the American War of
Independence and in the West Indies.

   She earned 'battle honours' for USHANT 1781 and ST.
VINCENT 1797 before her final honour of TRAFALGAR 1805 to
add to the ten 'honours' awarded to previous holders of the name:

ARMADA 1558, DOVER 1652, PORTLAND 1653, GABBARD 1653, SCHEVENINGEN 1653, ORFORDNESS 1666, SOLE BAY 1672, SCHOONEVELD 1673, TEXEL 1673 and BARFLEUR 1692.

In 1797 she was back in the Medway, this time converted as a hospital ship and crammed with hundreds of Dutch and French prisoners-of-war. After two years of this service she was to be turned to even more miserable a use as a prison hulk, but instead was returned (it is suggested upon Nelson's direct request, but more probably because of the loss through fire of the QUEEN CHARLOTTE – a 1st Rate built in Chatham in 1790) once more to the Dockyard and extensively rebuilt with a new, rounded bow; improved bowsprit rig and new carved figurehead; her lower gun deck was equipped with 32-pounders – fired by flintlocks instead of linstocks – instead of the original 42-pounders; magazines were relined and made safer; a sickbay provided (an innovation); the stern rebuilt with flat windows, and the ornate gallery removed; and 4,000 sheets of copper (weighing about 20 tons) fastened to the outer hull to provide protection from worm and weed damage.

Thus restored to her fighting condition at another cost of £70,933. She was commissioned in April 1803 and immediately sailed to Spithead and service as Nelson's flagship (with the hoisting of his Vice Admiral of the Blue flag on 18th May 1803) and ultimately to see battle at Trafalgar.

—Chatham Dockyard Historical Society
Research Paper No. 11: H.M.S. VICTORY
www.cdhs.org.uk

Some of the paperwork involved in the building of the original 1765 *Victory* has survived. Several letters may be found reproduced within the appendices to Chatham Dockyard Historical Society Research Paper No 30: BUILDING H.M.S. VICTORY.

Here is one such missive:

To the respective officers
Of His Majesty's Yard at Chatham

By the Principal Officers and Commrs. Of His Majesty's Navy

These are to direct and require you to Provide Masts and Yards for the Victory, building at your yard of the Dimensions mentioned on the other side, and the rigging and Blocks & to be agreeable to the enclosed Proportions as you have proposed.

The said ship to have 150 Tuns of Iron Ballast and an Iron Firehearth and Copper double Kettle suitable for a complement of 850 Men. The Sails, Anchors, and all other Boatswains and Carpenters' sea stores to be provided agreeable to the Warrant that will soon be sent you. For which this shall be your warrant.

Dated at the Navy Office 1st March 1764

G. Cockburn. Th. Brett E. Mason

While I was writing this story, evidence of the important roles played by women and children aboard the *Victory* was gleaned from renditions of life aboard by two celebrated artists. In the following painting 'The Death of Nelson' by Arthur William Davis, exhibited in the year 1807, we glimpse life on the Orlop Deck just after Lord Nelson was carried there for treatment.

In this painting we see one of ship's surgeons, William Beatty, attending the wounded Lord Nelson by lantern light. But if you look carefully into the shadows you find women at work. The woman pictured on the extreme left might easily be mistaken for Corrie Harriman on her way to relieve her brother on the Quarter Deck.

Unfortunately for those who served in 1805 it would be *fifty-four years after the battle* before another renowned painter Daniel Maclise, was commissioned to paint a huge fresco for the House of Lords depicting 'The Battle of Trafalgar.' Possibly inspired by Queen Victoria's determination to reward fighting women for their valor, Maclise was permitted to portray some of the *women and children* who fought in the battle. I have to thank Peter Sargison for bringing this significant work by Daniel Maclise to my attention.

Three images excerpted from Maclise's fresco may help the reader understand the shift in the public perception of children and women serving in the navy.

In Maclise's fresco the general public had their first glimpse of one of many hundreds of young children who served during the battle. In this heart-breaking portrait, what is that object the child is holding? Is it by any chance a tampion? Please write and tell me. You may reach me at *abarton@eastlink.ca*

Elsewhere in his splendid fresco Daniel Maclise depicted women tending to the rigging and seeing to the wounded during the battle.

Here Daniel Maclise depicted a female naval officer giving
an order at the very height of the battle. Notice that the officer
is wearing trousers. Only if dressed as a man was she allowed to
draw her pay. Such superstitions continue to plague women in our
own day.

After the battle, Cuthbert Collingwood, the surviving admiral,
made his report to the Admiralty in a fashion at odds with navy
tradition, writing that *'The ever to be lamented death of Vice Admiral Nelson who in the late conflict with the enemy, fell in the hour of victory...'*

On the receipt of Collingwood's report, news of Trafalgar
spread quickly, and Nelson's funeral was accompanied by a national outpouring of grief of a kind not to be matched until the
death of Princess Diana 192 years later.

Coming soon:

CORRIE'S WAR • BOOK 20
HOMEWARD BOUND!
CORRIE RETURNS!

Here is a sneak peek:

CHAPTER

CAPTAIN SIR CORRIE HARRIMAN stood on the Quarter Deck of the *Victory* peering at Chatham Dockyard. She could barely make out the Ropery for the mist, and there was no sign at all of Upnor Castle. She stamped her feet and beat her hands on her shoulders. Brrr! Despite the frigid air, she could hear the clatter and thumping that told her the shipwrights and foundry workers were hard at work nearby repairing the battered wrecks of His Majesty's ships after the battle off Cape Trafalgar. She could see several Spanish and French vessels captured during the engagement flying Britain's new Union flag, and found that a cheering sight here in the Medway.

Nelson's body had been brought home in a cask of brandy mixed with camphor and buried in a solemn ceremony at St. Paul's Cathedral in the City of London on the 9th of January. Corrie had attended the service and spied Mrs. Nelson, but had heard no word from the authorities of any settlement with regard to Emma Hamilton and Nelson's daughter Horatia. Apparently the mother and child were to be abandoned and left to fend for themselves. Corrie found that upsetting. She wished Nelson's dying wish had not been ignored by the government, but she was hardly surprised. The parliament consisted almost entirely of men. A few members would be women disguised as men, but there were probably not enough women to pull the political strings needed to help poor Emma and that little girl she and Nelson had conceived together. It was simply maddening.

Corrie turned her back on the Dockyard and examined the battered vessels waiting in line here in the Medway. The vessel she was searching for was her own frigate *Swift*. She had left the vessel in charge of her ageing sailing master Mr. Weevil three years ago. Was Weevil still alive? Was her *Swift* still in one piece? She bit her lip. Had her dear frigate been broken up for scrap or laid up in ordinary? It was perfectly possible. The Chatham officers worked for the Navy Board, not the Navy, and they had no love for Corrie Harriman, the officer who had had the audacity to *steal* the *Victory* from them. The officers of His Majesty's Yard strongly disapproved of Corrie. They had not received a penny in bribes for overseeing the refitting of the *Victory*, and considered that to be her fault, which it was.

Her eye lighted on a familiar arrangement of spars and rigging. Yes, here was her dear frigate. Apparently the *Swift* was still in one piece. But how small her former vessel appeared to Corrie now after her years of service in the *Victory*!

Anne came out on deck and stood by her side. 'They didn't break her up,' she said, leaning on her stick, and breathing heavily. That poisoned enemy pigeon had nearly killed her.

'Bring us alongside the *Swift*, Jensen, but allow for the turn of the tide,' Corrie said to her helmsman. 'Mr. Keeper, drop anchor when you are ready.'

'Aye, aye captain.'

Corrie hoped that the roar of the cable passing though the hawse hole would not be heard over the din of the working dockyard. She was feeling vulnerable. She had no wish to announce her arrival.

She was piped on board the *Swift* by a single side boy with a whistle.

'Mr. Weevil! It is good to see you again.'

'Welcome back, captain. Congratulations on your victory at Trafalgar. The whole town is talking about it. What a success!'

Corrie shook her head. 'We lost Nelson. I lost my father.'

Mr. Weevil's eyes filled with tears. He squeezed her hand. 'Your father was a fine, funny man.'

She lowered her voice. 'How soon can we sail, Mr. Weevil? Are we provisioned?'

'Aye, captain. Three months water, four months beef and pork in casks, all at the expense of the dockyard.'

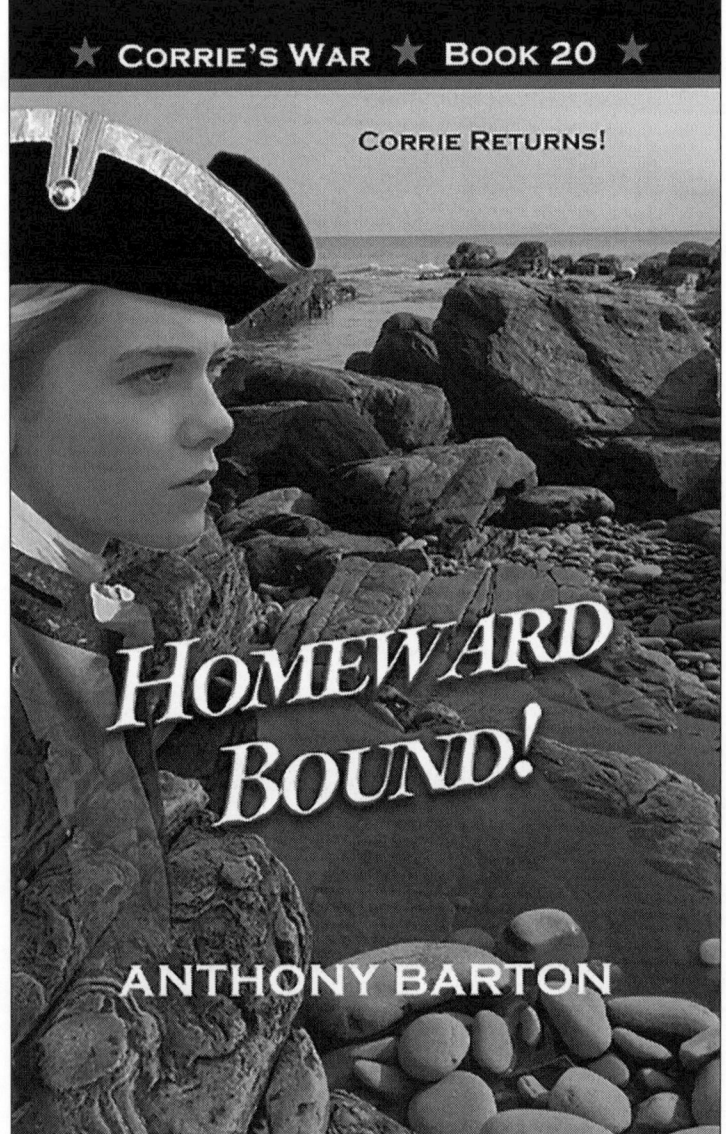

THE CORRIE'S WAR BOOKS

CORRIE'S WAR • BOOKS 1-4 • RUN OUT THE GUNS!

In the UK:

https://www.amazon.co.uk/dp/B07LDSXC53 for the e-book

https://www.amazon.co.uk/dp/1927721318 for the printed book

In the US:

https://www.amazon.com/dp/B07LDSXC53 for the e-book

https://www.amazon.com/dp/1927721318 for the printed book

In Canada:

https://www.amazon.ca/dp/B07LDSXC53 for the e-book

https://www.amazon.ca/dp/1927721318 for the printed book

In Australia:

https://www.amazon.au/dp/B07LDSXC53 for the e-book

https://www.amazon.au/dp/1927721318 for the printed book

CORRIE'S WAR • BOOKS 5-8 • BOARD THE ENEMY!

In the UK:

https://www.amazon.co.uk/dp/B07NHLNL1X for the e-book

https://www.amazon.co.uk/dp/1927721326 for the printed book

In the US:

https://www.amazon.co.uk/dp/B07NHLNL1X for the e-book

https://www.amazon.co.uk/dp/1927721326 for the printed book

In Canada:

https://www.amazon.ca/dp/B07NHLNL1X for the e-book

https://www.amazon.ca/dp/1927721326 for the printed book

In Australia:

https://www.amazon.au/dp/B07NHLNL1X for the e-book

https://www.amazon.au/dp/1927721326 for the printed book

CORRIE'S WAR • BOOKS 9-12 • CAPTURE THE FLAGSHIP!

In the UK:

https://www.amazon.co.uk/dp/B07R5GXYK4 for the e-book

https://www.amazon.co.uk/dp/1927721334 for the printed book

In the US:

https://www.amazon.com/dp/B07R5GXYK4 for the e-book

https://www.amazon.com/dp/1927721334 for the printed book

In Canada:

https://www.amazon.ca/dp/B07R5GXYK4 for the e-book

https://www.amazon.ca/dp/1927721334 for the printed book

In Australia:

https://www.amazon.au/dp/B07R5GXYK4 for the e-book

https://www.amazon.au/dp/1927721334 for the printed book

CORRIE'S WAR • Book 17 • STEAL THE VICTORY!

In the UK:

https://www.amazon.co.uk/dp/B07TFNFPF2 for the e-book

https://www.amazon.co.uk/dp/1927721350 for the printed book

In the US:

https://www.amazon.com/dp/B07TFNFPF2 for the e-book

https://www.amazon.com/dp/1927721350 for the printed book

In Canada:

https://www.amazon.ca/dp/B07TFNFPF2 for the e-book

https://www.amazon.ca/dp/1927721350 for the printed book

In Australia:

https://www.amazon.au/dp/B07TFNFPF2 for the e-book

https://www.amazon.au/dp/1927721350 for the printed book

Made in the USA
Monee, IL
29 January 2020